Our Bratty Queen

THE MEN OF PSYSPECOPS
BOOK 1

KAMERON CLAIRE

SNUGGLE WHORE PRESS, LLC

PSYSPECOPS

OUR
BRATTY
Queen
KAMERON Claire
USA TODAY BESTSELLING AUTHOR

Dedication

To all the Witty, Wicked & Wild Readers...
Never let them silence our Witty Tongues,
Never let them shame our Wicked Needs,
Never let them stop our Wild Deeds.
If it harm none, do what thy will!

Brat Kink

BDSM terminology is vast, varied, and often up to interpretation. For the purpose of this book, these definitions apply to our brat and brat tamers...

What is a Brat? In BDSM, a brat is a style of a submissive, usually rebellious or antagonistic to her Dominant with the intent of receiving attention and/or discipline. Outside of play, this can appear immature or childlike and often go hand-in-hand with DD/lg dynamics. Bratting often involves mini-challenges from the submissive to their Dominant like: back talk, questioning, resisting, refusing, whining, teasing, and other generally bratty behaviors.

What are Brat Tamers? Dominants who derive pleasure over "taming" a willful submissive who wants to give up control, but won't or can't without a fight—whether that fight is verbal or physical depends on the set hard limits. Additional limits to be negotiated and set are obedience and respect, as brats can and will poke at those boundaries as part of their play.

ENTES TUERE
PUNIRE IMPIOS

Chapter One

EPIPHANY

FOR THE FIRST time in months, I'm home and hiding from my ravenous fans. After years of endless scrutiny my career places upon me, I'm in desperate need of a couple of days away from the constant on-mode I have to don in front of the cameras.

I told my legion of faithful followers that I was taking a couple of spa days and promised to update them as soon as I could with all the goodies I'm pampered with while at this *ultra-reclusive* locale. They love when I gush about celebrity swag.

The truth is, I'm not at a luxury spa or an ultra-reclusive locale. I'm hiding in my apartment on the backside of my father's massive multi-million dollar estate.

My father is rich.

Not Elon Musk or Jeff Bezos rich, but I'm sure they attend the same parties. Last I checked, Daddy Dearest squeaked into the top four hundred of Forbes' richest men in America—somewhere in the two to three billion dollar range.

Yay for him.

Walter Krushner never remarried after his wife—my mother—died in a tragic car accident, but he's had plenty of women keeping his hotel beds warm.

Or, at least, that's what I assume.

Honestly, I wouldn't know since I'm never home. Even though I think he's a self-centered prick, I also believe he loved my mother and was truly heartbroken when she died that dreary fall evening ten years ago. I was twelve when she left us. Slick roads plus a drunk driver equals a hollow shell of a man going through the motions of being a human being. He was successful before she died, but her absence left a hole that he filled with corporate takeovers and billion-dollar mergers versus the care and welfare of his daughters.

Yep–daughters. Plural.

There's two of us, although I can't tell you what Leti is up to these days. It's been months since I've talked to her. Weeks since we've exchanged a text message. I guess since I'm home, I should call her. We could order lunch and hang out at the pool or some other sisterly activity we rarely do.

It's weird how that didn't occur to me until just now.

I guess, in some ways, I'm not much better than our Daddy Dearest.

Out of sight, out of mind.

By fourteen, I was modeling full time, and by sixteen, I had my own million-dollar enterprise growing as a social media influencer. I haven't been around to watch him conduct his days disconnected from his flesh and blood, or to witness my sister put her life on hold to be there for him if and when he finally pulls his head out of his ass.

My phone rings and disrupts the music streaming into my AirPods, which annoys me because I told my assistants I was unreachable this weekend.

I glance down at the screen and note the caller ID.

Speak of the absentee devil.

"Where are you?" My father's voice is sharp and to the point. I'm half surprised he knows my phone number, much less cares where I am.

"Hello, Walter."

"Epi, I'm in no mood for your attitude. Where are you?"

But I thought attitude-filled banter was how we showed affection in this family.

I sigh, "Not too far away. Why?"

"I need you to come home. Now."

It's only then that I notice my father's tone is off. "Why? What's going on?"

He exhales a heavy sigh, and I think I hear true weariness in his voice. "I think someone has kidnapped your sister."

I sit up with a start, knocking my iPhone off my lounge chair to the pool deck below. "What do you mean, you think?"

"I received a call and a demand for ransom. I haven't seen her in a while so I have no idea if this is real or not."

"Have you called the police?"

"Of course, I've called the fucking police! I'm not a complete moron. Where are you?" he barks.

I roll my eyes and pick up my phone from the ground. "At the pool—no more than two hundred yards from the house."

He blows out a sigh of relief. "Thank god you're safe. Come to my office."

"I'm on my way." I hang up my phone, only then digesting what he said.

Wait—Leti's been kidnapped?

Why?

How?

She doesn't go anywhere.

She doesn't do anything!

And outside of our father's money, she doesn't have anything.

Quiet as a church mouse—sweet, innocent, perfect little Leti isn't the type to cause anyone to pay her any attention. So, how the hell did she get herself kidnapped?

My heart beats faster as the reality of what my father has said spikes my fight-or-flight responses. I slip on a pair of shorts and my trainers, tuck my phone into my pocket, and jog to the back door of the house.

My sister and I are not close—despite the fact that we are identical twins.

Don't get me wrong. I love my sister in a distant rela-tive—the type you only see on major holidays—kind of way. We grew apart over the last eight years and, honestly, we have nothing in common.

I toured the country and then the world, modeling.

She, for all I know, sat in her room and did homework.

I became a brand spokesman for a cosmetics and athletic wear company before branding my own makeup and clothing lines.

She graduated high school early and went to a local university so she could continue to live at home. I still don't know what her degree is in—business, probably—but I know she works for one of our father's many companies. Doing what? I have no idea.

She's my polar opposite in so many ways, but that doesn't mean I don't love her.

I definitely don't want to see her hurt.

This doesn't make any sense. Who the hell would want to kidnap Leti?

Unless this is about our father's money? Maybe this is retaliation for a business deal gone bad? Could this be revenge for one of the hostile takeovers Walter has executed over the years?

I run up the back stairs and through the kitchen—ignoring the house staff—then around the stairwell, through the foyer, and into a large group of people.

No, not people.

Men.

Large men.

Massive men wearing suits and earpieces and—are those bulges in their jackets?

It's only when they turn their eyes on me that I remember I'm wearing a bikini top and very short shorts. I'm used to walking around near naked on a catwalk, bar top, dance floor, yacht deck and, of course, on stage, but for some reason—and maybe it's the way these men's eyes flash wide then harden when they turn to face me—I feel underdressed.

I search each one of their handsome faces—seven in total—and realize how serious this situation is.

One man's jaw tightens as we lock gazes.

His eyes are shrewd.

His expression is dismissive.

Which, in any other situation, would piss me off. I hate being underestimated.

"Epiphany Krushner?" One man steps forward to acknowledge me. He looks to be about twenty years older than the rest of the pack, but no less handsome—a silver fox, some would say—and oozing with authority.

"Who are you?" I look him up and down, something I do on autopilot now as part of my online persona.

"I'm Victor Townsend, owner of Townsend Security Agency. These men are members of my team."

I give everyone another cursory glance and stand tall despite my lack of clothing because I refuse to be cowered by any man. "Where's my father?"

"He's in his office with the FBI and his lawyers."

"Wait. What? How long ago—"

At that moment, my father walks out of his office. He looks like hammered shit—like he hasn't slept in days—and I notice the gray stubble peppering his normally clean shaven cheeks. "When did you get a phone call asking for ransom?"

"Let's go into the library." My father grips my upper

arm like he used to do when I was a kid and escorts me across the foyer into the giant library he had built for my mother twenty years ago.

I don't think I've been in this room since she died.

I pull my arm out of his grasp and turn around with my hands on my hips. "How long have you known Leti is missing?"

"Six hours."

"Six hours?" I glance at the men who followed us in here—their massive bulk dwarfing my mother's library with its floor-to-ceiling windows—and then back to my father. "You called the FBI, your lawyers, and a private security team before you called me?"

"What were you going to contribute to the situation?" My father huffs and runs his fingers through his thinning hair.

Honestly, I'm too shocked at first to speak. Yeah, I'm hardly ever here, but I'm no less present than he is, so that was a tad harsh, especially in front of an audience. I clench my fists at my sides, angry, hot tears building up behind my eyeballs. "Well, if I have nothing to contribute, then why did you bother calling me at all?"

Mr. Townsend steps forward again, his hand outstretched between us like a referee. "I asked him to call you, Ms. Krushner. We believe you're in danger."

"What?" I shake my head. "Why?"

"We found your sister's phone tossed in the bushes a few blocks from here. When the kidnappers called to demand a ransom, they used your name."

All the color drains from my face, which is not a good look for me. "I don't understand."

"You are identical twins, yes?"

"Yeah, but nobody who knows me would ever think we're the same..." I trail off as realization hits, and spin on my father. "You thought I was the one kidnapped? That's why you didn't call me."

My father lowers his voice. "I didn't have your phone number. You changed it six months ago and apparently didn't think your father needed your new one."

Wow. Our family dysfunction is on full display right now.

"Then I called Leti for your number, but obviously she couldn't answer her phone. For the last six hours, I've been missing two daughters."

I don't know what to say to that.

Do I feel guilty for making this harder on him than necessary because I didn't make it a point to give him my new number? A little.

But while I didn't offer, he didn't ask either.

The hot-as-fuck man with the shrewd eyes and the dismissive attitude speaks up. "Your five million followers —do they know you have a twin sister?"

"It's five point three million, thank you very much. And no, why would they?"

He effectively ignores my snark and continues. "So, it is reasonable to assume one of your followers could have seen Leti and mistaken her for you?"

I scoff. "My followers love me. We're talking about Swiffy fan base style loyalty. None of them would hurt me, and they certainly wouldn't call my father for ransom. Besides, sixty-eight percent of my fan base is teenage girls under the age of fifteen."

"And the other thirty-two percent?" He barely arches an eyebrow, his expression blank, which annoys the shit out of me.

"Why are you talking to me?" I huff, cocking my hip out and waving a dismissive hand in his direction.

One man coughs into his hand to smother a laugh, pissing me off more. The others continue to stare at me, stone-faced, like a group of natural-born killers.

Mr. Townsend speaks again. "Ms. Krushner, I would like you to meet Lee, the head of your security detail."

I glance at Mr. Townsend and then at Mr. Grumpy McHottie before turning to my father. "No. Absolutely not."

"Pip, be reasonable. Your sister is missing. I don't have the strength to worry about you, too." My father hasn't called me Pip in years. Not since my mother died.

The weakness in his voice knocks me down a few pegs.

"What aren't you telling me?"

Mr. Townsend speaks again. "The money requested for your sister—"

"Or you, as the case may be," Lee chimes in.

"—is significant, and the timeline given is unreasonable. It doesn't seem like the kidnappers are interested in a ransom. If we couple that with the probability they think they have you right now, that points to an overzealous fan who has zero intentions of releasing Leti. Ever."

All the feisty energy leaks out of me, and I sag into my mother's old reading chair in the corner of the room. Dear god, if anything happens to Leti because somebody is obsessed with me, I'll never forgive myself. She's spent her entire life avoiding trouble while I've run straight into it, guns blazing.

The gun, in this case, is my big fat mouth.

She doesn't deserve to be hurt because she looks like me.

I overhear my father say, "When can your team leave?"

Mr. Townsend responds, "We'll get started immediately."

"Wait. Who is going where?" I lift my head and put on my runway face. I learned a long time ago to never show weakness to anyone, ever, and it might make me come off looking like a cold bitch, but at least I'm not a weak one.

My father comes over and sits in the chair next to me. "These men are going after your sister while the other three take you to an undisclosed location until this is over."

"What if this is only about money? Are you sure this isn't someone pissed off at you for some corporate takeover thing in the past?"

"The FBI is looking into that, too," Mr. Townsend states.

My father takes my hand. "I know I haven't been

there for you, but I promise I'm going to do everything in my power to bring Leti home and keep you safe. The Townsend Security Agency is the best money can buy, and if they are recommending we do this, then this is what we should do."

"What's wrong with staying here?" My eyes travel over the men assembled. "We have a decent security system installed in this house."

My father raises his eyebrows. "How many parties have you had here? How many people have the code to the gate?"

"We can change that."

Lee steps forward and shakes his head. "The most secure location will be out of town, somewhere you've never been. According to your most recent posts, your followers believe you are taking a weekend sabbatical at a luxury spa. Correct?"

Holy hell, he's researched me? "Yes."

"Then we need to not be anywhere you've been before."

Scoffing, I jump out of my chair and throw my hands out at my sides. "For how long?"

"For as long as it takes to get your sister back and eliminate the threat," he growls back at me.

I spin around to face my father. "Daddy! I have a shoot this Wednesday."

Yes, it's a tactic I rarely employ, but it always works.

My father sighs. "Gentleman, surely there is a way to protect my daughter and impact her life as little as possible."

I spin back around to face all of them. I'll admit, I am not used to hearing no, and I definitely don't like hearing it now. "I have a business to run, appointments to keep, and endorsements to do. My fans expect to see me daily. Hourly, even."

Lee stares down at me, his face chiseled in stone. The only hint I have to any thought process going on in his head is the hard heat in his eyes. I swear, this man looks like he wants to beat me for being a petulant child, which only makes me want to act out more.

The phone in my father's office rings, disrupting our staring contest. My father jumps up and walks to his office faster than I've ever seen him move. I jog after him, pushing past another group of men in suits to stand by his side.

Someone hits a button and puts the call on speaker. My father says, "This is Walter Krushner."

A distorted voice screams on the other end of the line. "Why didn't you tell me I had the wrong daughter when we spoke this morning? Is this one even worth thirty million?"

My heart pounds in my chest with this revelation. I rush forward, slamming my hands down on the desk. "Let my sister go, you son of a bitch."

They meet my outburst with a moment of silence, followed by a mechanical, sinister chuckle. "Epi, Epi, Epi. I had no idea you had a twin. You've never mentioned her. Should I do to her all the things I was going to do to you?"

My father's voice cracks as he leans forward. "Don't hurt her. Please, we'll pay whatever you want."

The voice screams, "I wasn't talking to you!"

There's wrestling in the background, and I hear a distinctive slap of flesh against flesh as my sister screams. For the first time in I don't know how many years, I sink into my father's embrace, his arms wrapping tightly around me.

"It's amazing," the distorted voice continues. "She looks just like you, and yet, she's nothing like you. At first, I thought it was the difference between your public persona and the real you. It's the lack of a birthmark on her leg that clued me in. Do you know, she never once told me I was calling her by the wrong name? What kind of sister would risk torture to keep you safe when you've never publicly acknowledged her existence?"

Lack of a birthmark?

I glance up at my father, wondering if he remembers that my birthmark is high up on my inner thigh. My sister is not like me. She doesn't run around in bikinis. She certainly doesn't live on camera like I do. There's no way to see that birthmark is missing on her casually. They had to have stripped her, which—for someone like Leti— would be seriously traumatic.

Emotions I haven't felt in years and memories of our childhood before my mother died bubble up to the surface. We used to be so close. We did everything together, and I was often my sister's protector. I choke back a sob. "What do you want?"

"I wanted you and thirty million, but now I'm going

to apply an inconvenience fee of one hundred twelve million."

My father shakes his head. "It's Saturday afternoon. Even with my resources, it's going to take time to assemble one hundred forty-two million. We need more time."

"I'm going to give you plenty of time. I'm giving you seventy-two hours. At noon on Tuesday, I will call you again at this number and give you instructions on where to send my money. Oh, and let me be specific, I want $142,368,212.72. Did you write that down?"

The voice on the line chuckles. "I guess you don't need to, as you're recording this conversation. Don't think I don't know the FBI is there trying to trace my call. Good luck with that. I'll be in touch on Tuesday. Meanwhile, I'm going to get to know your other daughter."

The line goes dead. My father squeezes me tightly against his chest, running his hand up and down my back, trying to soothe me. It's only at that moment I realize I'm shaking, and maybe for the first time in my life, I'm truly scared.

ENTES TUERE
PUNIRE IMPIOS

Chapter Two

THE TOWNSEND MEN exit the office and walk across the foyer back to the library. I close the door behind us, my gaze bouncing between my team members, Case and Porter, before landing on Victor. "We've got to get her out of here. Now."

Victor nods. "Absolutely. The sooner the better. What did you see on the trace?"

We all turn to look at Soren, who is sitting at a small writing desk with his computer. He put a trace on Mr. Krushner's phone when the FBI wasn't looking because, as always, a pissing match started as soon as we walked in the door. Specifically, Reese started a fight so Soren could do his thing undetected.

We understand they have a job to do, but we do things a little differently, and require a fraction of the paperwork and none of the mother-may-I's. We also have one of the best hackers in the world on our team.

Soren shakes his head. "Whoever this is, they're

pretty good. The signal is bouncing all over the world. It doesn't sit in one place long enough to leave much of a fingerprint, but I'll get it. It's going to take me a bit to narrow it down."

"The location on Leti's phone stopped moving at six thirty-three this morning, so they could be three hundred miles from here by now. The first phone call was within minutes of the kidnapping, but this call came from a location where the kidnappers can mask themselves," I summarize, thinking about all the places they could be hiding her.

She could be anywhere. In six hours, they could have flown her out of the country if they had the means. Most kidnappers don't have the means, but considering Epiphany's international reach, anything is possible.

Soren's fingers fly over the keyboard. "That's a good point. Let me try something different."

"We also need to scan the audio for any background noise," Victor states.

"That's already happening," he says.

"Okay. While Soren's doing his thing, Reese—your team is on extraction. You should go to the garage and get everything ready. Lee—you, Case, and Porter have the princess. Good luck."

Reese and Caiden chuckle and slap me on the back.

Fuck, this is going to be one of the hardest missions of our lives. I'd take being shot at over babysitting a grade-A brat who, by the look of her, desperately needs to be tamed. I glance at Case and Porter and know their thoughts sync up with mine. As soon as she came jogging into the house in a bikini top that barely contained her full breasts, the chilled air pebbling her nipples—I knew we were in trouble.

Add in her snarky attitude and back talk?

Fuck, nothing gets me harder than making a brat submit, especially with a satisfied smile on her face.

I tilt my head in Porter's direction and he nods, walking out of the room without a word spoken. That's how it is between the three of us. We've known each other for fifteen years. Recruited in AIT, they sent us to the PsyOps qualification course, tested us individually, and then assigned us to a three-man team. We remained an active unit for twelve years and have seen a lot of combat—actually, we've seen a lot of everything. When I got shot three years ago and faced medical retirement from the Army, Case and Porter separated and join me in the civilian sector. Victor, who used to be our commander a half-dozen years ago, started the Townsend Security Agency and employs only ex-PsySpecOps operators— with our team being one of the first he recruited.

There's something about men who not only make it through the rigorous training, but also make a career of it. Our brains are wired a little differently. Whether society views that as a good or bad thing, I don't really give a fuck.

Case, Porter, and I are as close as brothers can be without sharing a womb. But we share everything else, including our women, and we've been looking for the one who will complete our family for a while now. When Victor called me this morning and told me to run a background check on Epiphany Krushner, I felt a spark I had every intention of burying deep. But then Case and Porter pulled their lazy asses out of bed, saw who I was researching, watched a handful of her YouTube videos with me, and we shared a look that meant trouble.

I'd hoped that when we met her in person, our initial attraction would fade, but then she had to be a smart ass—even more bratty than she is on camera—and I knew we were fucked.

Victor looks at me. "Are you taking her up north?"

Nodding, Case and I exchange another glance.

"We're taking her off grid," I say casually, knowing that being offline is going to send her over the edge.

Fuck me if I'm not looking forward to it.

"Something tells me this is going to take longer than expected," Reese says as he stands behind Soren, watching the ones and zeros fly across his computer screen.

"Unless you kill whoever the fuck is behind this during extraction," I say dryly.

Reese looks up with a treacherous smile. "One can fucking hope."

"Don't get shot." I rap my knuckles on the desk and chuck Case on the shoulder, tilting my head to the door. "It's time to get the princess packed up and on the road."

"You're the only one that gets shot." Reese shoots the low blow across the bow—referring to the time I got hit while on deployment—and lands a direct hit. If we weren't at a client's house, I'd take him to the ground for the slight, even a teasing one.

Instead, I shake my head and mutter under my breath, "Fuck off."

I can hear him snickering as I close the door.

Porter is standing in the foyer with Mr. Krushner and Epiphany. No, not standing. Arguing.

"Why are we standing here?" I say low, displeasure lacing my tone.

Porter takes one step back, rubbing his hand down his face in frustration.

"This has to happen," Mr. Krushner says to his daughter.

She stamps her foot against the marble floor. "But if this is an overzealous fan, I should be here to talk to them. Maybe I can change their minds? I'll give them swag bags or something."

I grab her arm, completely over this conversation. "We will escort you to your apartment so you can pack a small bag."

"And put on some clothes," Porter grumbles.

She glances down at my hand and then up at my face, her eyes narrowed and pouty lips pursed. I figure she's going to fight, but surprises me with, "Fine. Let's go."

I escort her out the front door and into our SUV before driving around the massive property to her apartment in the back. Porter jumps out of the truck to do a quick sweep of the property before running inside. Case, who sits in the back with Epiphany, stretches his arm over her to slam the door shut when she tries to exit the vehicle on her own.

I turn around to glare at her. "Let's get a couple of

things straight, Ms. Krushner. While you are under our care, you will do exactly as we say. You don't enter a room without us checking it first. You don't exit a vehicle without us clearing the area. Do you understand?"

Her jaw drops. "You can't talk to me this way."

I flash her a taunting grin. "Actually, I can. What's even better, Ms. Krushner, is I'm getting paid to do so. This can be easy, or this can be hard. It's entirely up to you."

Porter opens her door and offers his hand. "Everything's clear. Let's get you packed so we can go."

Case and I also exit the vehicle, but I give Porter another head nod and he goes with her inside the apartment.

Apartment, my ass. This place is bigger than most homes. Case and I do a lap around the structure, looking for anything out of the ordinary.

"What do you think?" Case asks, his gaze scanning every bush, every tree, every hiding place between here and as far as we can see.

My eyes are doing the same. "What do I think about what?"

"You know damn well what I'm talking about."

"No, I don't, because we're not having this conversation. We've taken on a new client, and our orders are very simple—keep her safe and hidden until we can rescue her sister and eliminate the threat."

"Yeah, our orders are simple, but spending time with her will not be."

I shake my head. "No other choice. This is what it is

and nothing more. The three of us will keep our cocks in our pants until this is over. End of discussion."

He lets out an exasperated breath. "I know you're right, but if she gives us even half the attitude she's given us so far, it's going to take everything within me not to bend her over my knee."

"Yeah." He's preaching to the choir. My hand has been itching since she ran nearly naked into a group of very large, very hard, very dominant men. If she was ours, her ass would already be bright red for flashing her shit in everyone's face.

A shrill scream pierces the air from the inside of the house. Case and I take off at a dead run through the front door with our weapons drawn. Porter walks towards us with his hands in his hair and shakes his head, his jaw clenched tight. I look past him down the hallway at Epiphany, pacing back and forth in her bedroom while pitching a fit.

"She's freaking out because I told her she couldn't bring her computer," Porter snarls.

Case laughs. "Dude, she lives her life online. Of course, she's going to have a fit."

I lower my voice. "Where we're going there is no internet, but she doesn't need to know that. We'll put her stuff in the lead-lined box in the trunk to disrupt the signal. She'll never be the wiser."

Staring down the hallway, I take a deep breath and square my shoulders. "I'll go get her. Porter, you're with the truck."

"Roger that." He sounds almost relieved.

Case's footsteps fall in line behind me as I stomp down the hallway. As soon as I get to her room, I use my booming command voice. "What the hell is the hold-up?"

My tone has the desired effect, causing her to jump and spin around with wide eyes. "Jesus, you scared me. Why are you yelling?"

I narrow my eyes. "That was not yelling. You'll know when I'm yelling. This is my patience coming to an end. You've pissed off Porter, the nicest of the three of us, so what does that tell you?"

She pouts. "He said I couldn't bring any of my stuff."

"What exactly do you need while you're hiding from your would-be kidnappers who are currently torturing your sister?"

She has nothing to say to that, and for half a second actually looks embarrassed. Then she presses her lips together and turns her back to me, mumbling under her breath. "But I have a business to run."

"Ms. Krushner, you need to get your priorities straight. You are in danger. Your sister is in peril. And now you have three minutes to grab whatever clothes and toiletries you need to last you two weeks. In three minutes and two seconds, I will drag you out of here with whatever you have packed. If all you remember to throw in your bag is underwear, then that's what you will live in until this is over. Do I make myself clear?" I set a timer on my watch to emphasize my point.

"Fine." She huffs and goes to a drawer, chucking clothes onto her bed. Red lace panties fly through the air.

I turn my back to her and catch a shit-eating grin on Case's face.

"No," I hiss.

He chuckles and walks down the hallway, pushing open the door of another bedroom. "Check this out."

I leave my post and stop beside him, getting an eyeful of various production equipment. Someone retrofitted the room as a studio set with lights and multiple cameras to photograph every angle. Nothing is private or sacred in this room. She has a makeup table in front of one set of cameras and a changing screen in front of the others.

This morning, we watched a few videos of her testing out new products and doing her makeup, as well as changing clothes and modeling them for the camera, but the room in those videos was different, which means she has several locations she broadcasts from.

"Here." She shoves a Louis Vuitton duffle bag into Case's arms. "I understand I won't be able to tell my fans where I am, or what is going on, but you don't have to worry about me giving away our location."

I raise my brow. "Why is that?"

"Because I have a scrambler that masks my IP address."

This gets my attention. "You do?"

"Yes. My IT guru—well, I guess she's my ex-IT guru now—designed it for me a year ago when this weird guy showed up at all of our live locations."

"Ex?" I ask.

"Weird guy?" Case tacks on.

She frowns in that way that looks remorseful, but isn't. "Yeah, I had to fire her."

I nod, my insides telling me it's time to get on the road. "Grab it and the bare minimum, and let's go."

She flashes a genuine smile, and it hits me harder than it should. She's really beautiful, and while her bratty behavior turns me on, this tugs at another part of me. I wouldn't mind seeing her smile often. "I knew you'd be reasonable. And you say Porter's the nice one."

Case chuckles darkly. "Oh, he is."

She stares at him for a second before turning and filling an LV train case with beauty supplies. Then she grabs her laptop, iPad, a traveling eighteen-inch ring light and a thin, four-port hub, shoving them all into a bag of cables.

I point to the last piece of equipment. "Mind if I look at that?"

"Sure." She hands it to me.

It's a basic, fifty-dollar Netgear hub, but the tamper seal has been broken. I hand it back to her and nod. "Okay. Let's go."

I grab her equipment bag while Case leads us out of the house with her three thousand-dollar duffle bag hanging off his shoulder. Porter has the back door open, ushering her into the truck as Case and I store her stuff in the trunk. I pull the hub out of the bag and lower my voice. "We'll swing by the front and give this to Soren."

He nods.

I slip her laptop and iPad into a lead-lined box we keep in the trunk for this exact situation, and then remember her cell phone. Fuck, how am I going to pry that out of her hands without a fight?

As if he's reading my mind, Case speaks up. "Ms. Krushner—we need to swing by the house and have Soren scan your phone to make sure it's clean."

"Whatever," she huffs, handing her phone to Porter without a fight.

"Good thinking," I mutter.

He grins. "You're the boss, I'm the brains, and Porter's the pretty one."

"I thought you were the brute?"

"Yeah, I'm that, too."

ENTES TUERE
PUNIRE IMPIOS

Chapter Three

CASE

I JUMP out of the SUV at the front of the house and run in to catch Soren as he's packing up his bag of tricks. "Her ex-IT person designed her this *scrambler*. Do you want to check it out?"

"Absolutely." He takes it from my hand and tucks it into his laptop bag.

"Are you leaving?" I look around for Reese and Caiden, but Soren is by himself in the library.

"Yeah. We're heading back to the garage. I think I have a lock on Leti southwest of here near Peoria. I'll look at this *scrambler* while the guys are packing up the tactical gear."

"Are you going with them for extraction?"

He nods casually, but I notice the side eye he gives me. "Yeah, the signal's too erratic to not be tracking her constantly."

Dammit. That was a stupid question, and I shouldn't have asked because, of course, he's going—he's part of the team. Soren is as skilled as the rest of us, but not nearly as bloodthirsty, which means men like me underestimate him sometimes—except, in this case, I know better. He's got brains and talent the rest of us can only sit back and marvel at, but I know for a fact he can kill a man just as easily as the rest of us. My dumb ass should remember that just because he isn't hotheaded like me, that doesn't make him any less lethal.

I would apologize, but I know he doesn't want to hear it.

I hand him Epi's cell phone. "Can you make this seem like it's working, but take it offline and route all the traffic internal to us?"

Chuckling, he accepts the phone. "Is she giving you hell already?"

"You have no idea."

"Yeah, but you guys like shit like that. Chicks with a ton of attitude make you hard."

I roll my eyes and mutter again, "You have no idea."

"They are beautiful, aren't they?" Soren says casually as he pops out the SIM card and slides it into a home-made handheld device—one of his many whiz bang tech gadgets. He then opens an app on his phone, also created by him, and ninety seconds later, slides the SIM card back into her phone and hands it to me.

The man is a fucking genius with technology.

With normal people who aren't hard, twisted little fucks like me and the rest of our brethren—not so much.

"Yeah, they're beautiful." My thoughts go to the sister who is going through god knows what right now. I hope they get to her in time. Nothing boils my blood faster than coming across a brutalized woman, and I don't begrudge Reese's team being the one on extraction. If they walk into a messy scene, it won't go well for the men who caused the mess, which is the only part I'm sad I'll miss.

I hold up the phone. "Thanks. You guys be careful out there."

"You'll hear from us when we have something." He hoists his computer bag up on his shoulder.

"Same." I tilt my chin as I catch Victor's eye before exiting the property. The FBI agents mad-dog Soren and me from their perch in Mr. Krushner's office. I don't envy Victor having to deal with them. It's his twenty-plus years of Army officer politics that gives him the strength of character to navigate their bullshit. Meanwhile, he knows we're the ones in the shadows getting the real job done, minus the bureaucracy and red tape. That's the number one reason billionaires and the government pay us loads of cash to do the things law enforcement can't do.

We keep their hands clean and consciences clear.

I slide into the backseat next to our brat—dammit, I mean, client—and hand over her cell phone. "All clean, sweetheart."

"I knew it would be." Her gaze lingers on me for a heartbeat longer than appropriate, diverting blood that should feed my brain to my dick. I can't stop my gaze from raking over her. She put on a thread-bare V-neck T-shirt over her bikini top, but didn't bother putting on longer pants, leaving miles of leg and smooth, tempting flesh for me to lust after on the short drive to our place in the old industrial area of downtown.

As soon as Lee pulls onto the highway, I ask one of a dozen questions bouncing around in my head. "Tell us more about this ex-IT guru."

She shrugs, her fingers flying over her phone's keyboard, her eyes glued to the screen. "What's there to say? She's super smart, but when I chose not to invest in her brilliant business idea, she got weird. I guess the right word would be aggressive—passive-aggressive—and I don't need or want that kind of energy in my inner circle. So, I fired her."

"How long ago was that?" Porter turns around and makes eye contact with me before sliding his eyes toward her.

We're in sync, as always. There is more to this story. Maybe even more than Epi realizes.

"I don't know, maybe six months." She looks up from her phone to flash him a warm smile that provokes a tinge of jealousy within me. For reasons unknown, I want her to smile at me. Actually, I want to see her light up when I enter a room or, better yet, make her come.

Fuck, this is going to be the longest mission of my life if I can't squash the filthy thoughts running through my head.

"In your last Instagram post, you told your fans you were going to a spa. Did you ever mention where?" Lee asks, his eyes also meeting mine in the rearview mirror. That's the thing about the three of us; we damn near share a brain. Anything he's thinking, I'm probably also thinking. It's why we work so well as a team.

"I said it was a super-secret tropical resort—the kind you have to be invited to. That was my excuse for being offline." She waves her hand in the air. "Too busy mingling with celebrities and all that, ya know?"

Lies. Just like everything else online, a bunch of fucking lies. I wonder how much of her personality is built on bullshit and how much of it is real?

"Did anyone in your entourage know you were really going to be here in Chicago?" I ask.

Her head snaps up, and she turns bewildered eyes on me, like what I've asked is pure stupidity. "No one. Trust me, in this business, the draw is the illusion I create for my fans, and there are too many gossips around to not hold my truth as close as possible."

Lee pulls into the secure garage underneath the downtown building we bought two years ago. On the outside, it looks damn near abandoned. There is no yard or anything to give it a homey feel. But it's solid and practically indestructible, and nobody bothers us in the middle of the industrial neighborhood.

"Where are we?" Epi curls her lip in disgust.

"Our place. We need to pack a couple of bags ourselves." I open my door at the same time Porter opens hers.

"Can't I wait in the car?" she whines, looking around as if something on the ground is going to jump up and bite her. What she doesn't realize is the only things prepared to bite her ass are the three men protecting her.

"Nope. Outside of using the bathroom, you will not be out of our sight until this is over. Don't worry; this won't take but a few minutes." Porter offers her his hand.

She huffs and takes it, letting him escort her from the truck.

We will travel in two vehicles up to the safe house. Porter and I will drive the second one while Lee drives the front vehicle with Epi sitting in the backseat. Most threats come from the rear, and while I'm driving, Porter will be my tactical eyes and ears.

Because we're always ready to go, it takes less than five minutes to change out of my suit, grab my go bag plus my tactical gear, and meet everyone in the living room.

"Wow," she muses. "This place is a lot nicer on the inside."

"Sometimes it's beneficial to have people underestimate you by what they see on the outside," I point out.

She scoffs, "Not in my line of work."

Lee stops what he's doing and turns to look at her. "And how much of your life is not online?"

"None. It doesn't pay to be offline. Online is where my money comes from."

I drop my bag to the ground and ask the one question that's been bothering me the most. "Why don't your fans know you have a twin sister? Are you ashamed of her?"

She spins on me, anger flaring to life in her eyes. I'd be lying if I said poking at her doesn't turns me on. "My sister doesn't like to have attention on her. I'm not ashamed of her, although I'll admit I don't know her very well anymore. It's out of respect for her privacy that I don't tell people about her."

"Respect?" I quip.

"Who in your world knows about her?" Lee asks, throwing me a look that says *chill out*. He knows I'm poking at her on purpose, and getting off on her responses that are dripping with venom.

"No one. She and I lived very different lives after our mother died, and there was no reason to talk about her when she's not a part of my social circle." Epi plops down on the couch and crosses her arms over her chest. "I know I sound like a real bitch right now. I love my sister—I would do anything for her if she asked—but we have nothing in common. We handled our mother's death differently. She clung to our father—not that he noticed—and I took the opportunity of having no one watching after me to get away from that tomb of a home and take care of myself."

She narrows her eyes at me. "I'll do whatever I have to do to bring Leti home—which is the only reason I'm going along with any of this security detail BS—and while I feel horrible that this happened to her, this is not my fault, and I don't appreciate you trying to make me feel bad about it."

The way she digs in her heels, the contempt for me in her expression right now—fuck, I'm a sick and twisted man because all it does is make me hard. I glance at Lee, his eyebrow raised at me in question, and then at Porter, who watches this exchange from the kitchen with a contemplative look on his face, before shaking my head and turning away to give up the fight.

For now.

TEN MINUTES LATER, we pull onto the interstate and drive north in a second vehicle behind Lee.

Porter finally breaks the silence. "She's something else, isn't she?"

"That's describing her mildly."

"So, you feel it, too?"

Nodding, I don't take my eyes off the road. "So does Lee. Not that we can do shit about it, given the situation."

"I wonder how crazy she's making him right now?" Porter muses.

I chuckle. "Two hundred bucks says as soon as we stop at the cabin, he takes a walk."

"As soon as we get there? You don't think he can hold his shit together for longer than that?"

I shake my head, my grin spreading into a full-blown smile. What Porter doesn't know is that her phone is bound to stop working while on the drive, which means she'll have nothing better to do than to needle Lee. I have no doubt she knows what she's doing to us with her quick tongue and bratty attitude. Maybe she doesn't realize how much it works for us—that we are sick fucks who get off on a bratty submissive who taunts, teases, picks, and pokes until we tame her—but she knows she has our attention in more than one way, and she likes it that way. "Nope. Two hundred bucks. Take it or leave it."

"All right, you're on."

My phone rings, and I hit the button on the steering wheel. "Yeah?"

"Hey," Soren's voice plays over the car's audio system. "We've got a lock on Leti's location and are heading there now. Meanwhile, I took a quick look at this little Netgear hub, and while they programmed it to scramble the originating IP address, it's also got a little GPS tracker inside of it. Whoever's on the other side of this knows where this little hub is at all times, and if Epiphany has been carrying it with her, it's been giving somebody her location within half a mile or better every time she plugs it in."

"Interesting. That explains how they knew she was at her father's residence."

Soren huffs, like we're not grasping the full impact of this revelation. "It's better than interesting. It's because of this little hub that we know where we're going, since it popped hot at the location I'd triangulated off the phone call."

"That's fantastic, man," I say, checking my mirrors and then glancing at Porter. "Who's in the car with you right now?"

"What's up?" Caiden says right before Reese also announces himself with a simple, "Yo."

Porter scrolls through the notes on his phone. "The designer of this little hub is a woman, Claudine Humphrey—an ex-employee of Ms. Krushner's. From the story Epi told us, she's most likely a hostile ex-employee with an axe to grind."

"A woman? That's not the typical M.O. of a kidnapper," Caiden says.

"No, but something she said has me thinking. The dollar amount demanded is so specific. Ms. Krushner said she fired Claudine when she didn't glom onto a business opportunity presented to her. Maybe one hundred and forty-two million is the expected gains of said transaction?"

"Did you ask the client about this?" Soren asks.

"No, not yet."

Porter interjects. "If it's a woman behind this, she has to have male partners. Even though the twins aren't much to handle, how many women do you know who could wrangle a woman to the ground and then inflict bodily harm?"

Reese responds dryly, "There are some out there."

My mind spins with the possibilities. "Damn, I've never popped a woman before."

I glance again at Porter to make sure I'm not forgetting somebody, but he shakes his head. All of our years of combat, neither one of us has ever had to draw our weapons on a female. We've had to detain some. Frisk and hold—and not in the pleasurable way—but we've never squared off against one.

"They bleed just the same as men," Reese continues without a hint of emotion in his tone, telling me exactly where his head is at.

I shrug. "Whatever it takes."

"Exactly. We'll call you guys tonight, after it's done."

We disconnect the call, and I drum my thumbs against the steering wheel, realizing this job may be over before it starts. "We might head home before we unpack."

"Is that a good or a bad thing?" Porter asks.

I raise my eyebrow and say nothing, but in my head I'm thinking *both*. Time spent with Ms. Epiphany Krushner could be immensely pleasurable, even though it technically can't happen given the circumstances that brought us together, and yet, something tells me she's going to make our lives a living hell over however many days we're stuck together.

We'll like it, even as we hate it.

"Come on. She's fucking hot and sassy, and my palm has been itching to connect with her flesh since she came bouncing into the house."

I chuckle at that statement. "Damn, if you want to spank her, she's got to be bad. You usually leave that to me and Lee."

"Not bad—just a brat. A delectable, mouthy, brat with the plumpest fucking lips—"

"Been thinking about her mouth, have you?"

He nods, his fist clenched against his thigh. "Man, when she started pitching a fit in her apartment, it took everything within me not to rip my belt out of its loops."

I laugh, hitting the turn signal to follow Lee off of the interstate. "Well, this could be over tonight, or it could take two weeks, so I suggest you focus on something else for the time being. Otherwise, you're going to have to walk around with the worst case of blue balls."

"Like she doesn't make you hard?" he snips back.

"She does, but we have a job to do."

"I can protect her life and daydream about bending her over a counter at the same time."

"Fuck, Brother. That is not an image I need in my head right now."

"You're welcome," he says lightly, but one look at his face, his eyes glued to his side mirror, proves there is nothing humorous going on in his head.

"What is it?" I glance at both of my mirrors.

"Tan van, three cars back. They've been loosely following us for a while."

I search my side mirror again, visually confirming the van in question. "Call Lee. We need to make a pit stop."

He nods. "On it."

ENTES TUERE
PUNIRE IMPIOS

Chapter Four

EPIPHANY

"MY PHONE'S NOT WORKING. What back-ass country hovel are you taking me to?"

I slump against the backseat and throw my phone on top of my bag. Crossing my arms over my chest, I glare at Lee through the rearview mirror. We've been driving forever, or so it seems, and I'm restless. I'm used to traveling all over the world, so it's not the time in the car that's driving me crazy. It's the big, sexy, broody man who refuses to entertain me, and, without my phone, I'm at a complete loss as to how to distract myself from the seriousness facing my family.

No, Leti and I aren't close, but she is my sister, and I can't sit here and dwell on what she's going through right now. If my mind spins in that direction, I'll fall apart, and that is something I refuse to do in front of these strange men, no matter how delicious they are.

I barely allow myself to fall apart when I'm alone, but I never break down in front of others.

Never.

"You told the world you were taking a long-needed break. Sit back, relax, and pretend like you're on vacation."

"Vacation? This is not what I'd call a vacation. Where's my mojito and bare-chested, sun-kissed server in white linen pants slung low on his waist?" I flash a taunting smirk at Lee's scowling reflection.

His eyes rest on me for a long minute before dismissing me as they return to the road, but it's when his gaze flicks back to me that I get an idea of how I can entertain myself. I dig through my bag, find my AirPods, and put them in my ears. Then I bring up my music app and find a sexy playlist.

Dancing in my seat, I close my eyes and pretend to let the music take me over, gyrating my hips against the leather interior. I bring my arms up and run my fingers through my hair, piling it high on my head as I sing softly to the chorus. My tongue darts out of my mouth between verses, and then I suck in my bottom lip, and even though I'm putting on a show like I have a million times before, grinding my pussy against the seat makes my shorts ride up and rub against my clit, which is a whole new vibe to work with.

Damn, I probably should have put on my yoga pants.

I open my eyes and catch his glare in the mirror. Again, he says nothing.

Ugh! Now I'm bored, antsy, and a bit turned on—and this guy is giving me nada, nothing, zilch to feed off of.

Since I was fourteen, I've been partying with people

older than me. I know it sounds terrible—and now, as a twenty-two-year-old, I think so, too—but back then I learned how to get my way through any means necessary. My father's money saved me from some of the ugly experiences in life. The *chaperones*—I use that term loosely—he hired did the bare minimum to keep me from being violated or put in jail. Otherwise, they were sitting next to me, down to party with the who's who of the rich and famous.

I've hopped on an Arab prince's jet to an exotic location one night and then come back two weeks later to party on a yacht docked off the coast of San Diego. I've attended red carpet events on the arm of some up-and-coming actor one weekend before drinking champagne with a senator's son the next. I've been proposed to by a half-dozen men twenty to forty years older than me, and if money and stability could satiate this need burning deep within my belly, I would have taken one of them up on it just to cut the last remaining tie to my father.

But none of those men could give me what I crave most—the security I need to be vulnerable for once in my life. None of them look deep enough to see what I really need to be me. Every single one of them allows me to do whatever I want, whenever I want, no matter how outlandish—as if allowing me to get away with murder would make me love them or something? They want to cage me, but by marriage and money, not by love and affection. They view me as a possession to flaunt or a challenge to overcome, nothing more. I know if I married any of them, they'd have placed me on a pedestal to be admired, but not truly played with—which is what I desperately want more than anything.

There's a difference between being viewed as a trophy and treasured as a prize.

I'm over people handing me things.

I'm tired of being the center of attention and yet utterly ignored.

None of my fans—or *entourage*, as Case called them —really know me.

Hell, at this point, I'm not sure I would recognize the real me. What I do know is the real me wouldn't keep millions of ravenous fans glued to their phones, clicking my Buy Now links.

And so, when facing my audience, I'm the fun, ultimate party girl who is down for anything reasonable and pseudo-responsible. Unlike the epic party girls before me —Lindsay, Paris, Brittney, and Kim—I have no intention of becoming notorious, although I have been advised on more than one occasion that flashing the paparazzi my bare pussy might gain me a few million more followers.

No thank you.

I'm good with my number of fans and their demographics. Most of them are young, completely harmless girls learning about makeup and fashion. If I grow to the next level of fandom, I'll have to employ a full-time security team—something I definitely don't want. I'm comfortably on the cusp of said event, but a kidnapping scandal will surely put a million more eyes on me.

The kind of eyes I don't want.

I meet Lee's gaze in the mirror, my lips curling in

triumph as I pull my AirPods out of my ears. "Do you like what you see?"

The lines around his eyes tighten, but again, he says nothing.

I slump forward in defeat and whine, "I'm bored. Can't I come sit in the front seat with you?"

"Absolutely not," he says sharply.

I unbuckle my seat belt and lean forward, squeezing my arms and chest between the two front chairs, and draping myself over the center console. "Are you going to be a stick in the mud all weekend?"

He glances at me, his eyes trailing over my face and down to my cleavage on full display in this loose shirt. Then he drags them back up to the road, the muscles in his jaw flexing as he speaks. "Sit back and put on your seatbelt."

"If I don't?" I raise my brow in challenge.

His hands tighten on the steering wheel, and I swear I hear his molars grinding together.

I continue to whine softly. "Don't you understand? I need a distraction. Why don't you tell me a story or something?"

"Sure," he quips. "One time, there was a woman in trouble, but instead of accepting the help provided to her, she tormented her would-be saviors, giving them ideas about taking her into the woods and tying her to a tree."

"Ohhh! Like a public beating or shaming or something?" I croon, grinning when his entire body tightens.

"Motherfucker," he hisses, his eyes glued to the road ahead of us.

I sit back and do a little dance in my seat because now I know how I'm going to entertain and, more importantly, distract myself this weekend. What I'm going to do, specifically, I don't know yet. It seems that being a contrary handful, and general pain in the ass works on these guys... so I guess that's what I'll do.

Wow, it's like I've been training for this my entire life.

And let's face it, my security team is hot.

Actually, all the men, including the silver fox boss, are attractive. Big and broad, each one of them filled out his suit jacket perfectly. It's obvious they keep themselves in great shape. When we stopped at their place and they changed clothes—each one of them decked out in form-fitted black T-shirts, utility pants, and boots—they scream Hollywood action hero sex appeal.

I'm curious about their living situation. I mean, how do three testosterone-laden men live together? Is that abandoned warehouse their full-time home or a place in the city where they crash and keep their gear during the week, only to retreat to their private spaces on the week-ends? If it is their primary residence, how do they date? The upstairs had bedrooms and, presumably, bathrooms, but otherwise, the main floor above the garage was a wide open floor plan with no privacy.

Maybe they are together?

Like *together* together.

Three super sexy men... I suppose it's possible.

Unfair to women, but totally plausible.

I stare at Lee's reflection, taking in the sharp angles of his face. He has a strong nose and a mid-length beard.

Longer, dark sandy brown hair curls up at his neck, and I'm betting if he hung out in the sun, it would lighten to a dark blonde. He's got brown eyes, slightly darker than his hair, and a prominent vein in his forehead that seems to get more pronounced around me.

Maybe I'll cause him to have an aneurysm before this is over?

It won't be the first time I've been told I was going to be the death of someone.

Case has a youthful face, but also a scar down his left eye and over his cheek that takes away any boyish charm. He's leaner than Lee—not nearly as wide, but still plenty big. I'd say he's at least six-two, maybe taller. Although his scar could be a distraction to some, because he has the most piercing blue eyes I've ever seen, I think it is more of a distinction. Add the brilliance of his irises to the small cleft in his square, clean-shaven jaw, and the man has no problem attracting whatever attention he desires.

But Porter?

Good god, Porter.

If he wants to change careers, I know a dozen photographers who would love to get their lenses and other things on him. He's got dark hair, smooth, chiseled features, and gray eyes that smolder at all times. And he has the plumpest lips made for kissing and whatever else he wants to do with them. Just thinking about them has me squirming in my seat again.

I can imagine these three falling into bed together, and yeah... I've seen my fair share of gay porn, and while those guys are always gorgeous, these three could make serious bank.

Again, I know people. Maybe I should offer to make a few connections for them?

"What?" Lee growls, startling me out of my salacious thoughts. It takes a minute for me to realize he's talking to whoever is in his head via the little earpiece I noticed they all wear.

"How do you have a cell signal and I don't?" I scoff, grabbing my phone and checking the screen again.

"Where?" His gaze flicks to me and then back to the road. "There's a scenic lookout two miles ahead. We'll pull over there."

He turns to me, his expression grim. "Put on your seatbelt. Now."

Although he's always direct, there's something about his tone that tells me not to fuck with him on this. I snap my seatbelt in place, glancing over each shoulder to look out of the windows. "Is something wrong?"

"We're pulling off for a quick break, but you will stay in the car."

"But—"

"Ms. Krushner, I will handcuff you to the fucking seat if you do not obey me." He pulls the vehicle off the road and puts it in park, but leaves the engine running. His body is tight and primed like a warrior sizing up the enemy, but as I look around, all I see are the men in the other vehicle and no one else.

"Obey?" I blurt.

Unbuckling his seatbelt, he turns to me with his

hand on the door handle. "These windows are blacked out and bulletproof. However, I'd appreciate it if you'd lie down."

I hunker down despite my lack of understanding. "But—"

"Good girl." He slips out of the car, pulling his gun from its holster and tucking it into the back of his pants. Closing the door, I hear the door locks engage.

Good girl? I don't know why, but I like hearing those words from his lips. I peek out the side window and then out the back as Lee, Case, and Porter meet between the vehicles. They have their eyes trained on the road, watching as each car passes, but what they are looking for, I don't know.

Seeing these men stand together as a tightly formed group, visibly animated in their conversation, there's something powerful and strangely sexy about the three of them. I bet when they're on their downtime, they make women swoon with their dominant personalities.

But how could a girl choose?

Each one is panty-melting in his own way.

Lee puts his hand behind his back and grips his weapon as an old, tan van slows down before speeding away.

Is that why we pulled over?

Is somebody following us?

I pull on the door handle, intent on jumping out to ask what's going on, but the door doesn't budge. Then I see the murderous glint in Lee's eye as he glances at the SUV, fully aware of what I tried and failed to do.

Feeling silently reprimanded, I sag against the back-seat and use my bag as a pillow.

This sucks.

Even though I want to be coveted and controlled, I don't like being told what to do—or more to the point, I don't like being left behind or told no. I especially don't like hearing the word no. I need to schedule an appointment with my therapist because even I don't understand what I want or need most days.

All I know is I have an ache inside of me that has never come close to being soothed by the boyfriends I've had.

What do I want that I don't already have thrown at my feet?

ENTES TUERE
PUNIRE IMPIOS

Chapter Five

PORTER

"SHOULD WE FOLLOW THEM?"

Lee curses under his breath. "If we do and they're some random couple out on a joyride, we're not only wasting time and scaring the shit out of some townies, but we leave her exposed for longer than necessary."

"They have a giant antenna on top of their van. They're not some random couple out on a fucking joyride." I bitch through clenched teeth, aggravation coursing through my veins. This is bullshit. We should go after them. We could wrap this up in minutes if those are the kidnappers, or even a faction of the villainous kidnapping team. It's not that I don't want to make it to the cabin, secure our client, and spend some time getting to know her—because I do. Otherwise, how would a man like me meet a woman like her?

But every moment that passes without finding and securing her sister is a minute where things can go from bad to worse. And having an emotionally broken woman on my hands is the last thing I want—especially while indecent thoughts of sliding deep into her body keep crossing my mind.

I should be ashamed of myself.

Let me be clear—I am not.

Lee shakes his head. "Lots of people use hand radios out here. There isn't a cell tower within fifty miles of the cabin and we're getting close."

"We know this ex-IT chick placed a tracker on Epi once before. Who's to say there's not more?" Case points out.

"Fuck." Lee mutters and stares down the road after the van, which tells me he's dying to chase them down, too.

Dammit. Now's the time to do it. In another thirty minutes, the sun will dip below the horizon and our visibility will diminish. If Epi wasn't in the car, we'd already be nudging them off the road with a couple of strategic taps to their bumper.

He continues. "All of her shit is in my vehicle, so we'll move her to yours. If there's a tracker in her stuff, I'll take them on a wild goose chase while you secure her at the cabin. Are we sure Soren fixed her phone?"

"I have a log of her activity on my cell and she hasn't gotten one single reply, which I bet is annoying the shit out of her," Case says.

"You have no idea." Lee rolls his eyes and looks over his shoulder as the locks on the vehicle click like they do when someone attempts to open a secure door.

"I'm surprised she hasn't jumped out to join us," I say

with genuine curiosity. It's not like she's followed any of our other directions without complaint, so why would she comply with this one?

"I engaged the child-safety locks and locked her in after I got out of the vehicle," Lee grumbles.

"We should probably frisk her in case there's a tracker sewn into her clothes or tattooed on her body." I joke, trying to lighten Lee's mood.

The van's gone, so the moment is over for me, but he's going to be in a pissy mood all night. I can tell after fifteen years with the man.

He gives me a look that tells me he's not amused. "I can't wait for you to spend a couple of hours with her."

"Oh, that reminds me." Case snaps his fingers. "Let's say this side adventure hadn't happened, and we made it to the cabin without issue—"

"Yeah?" Lee runs his hand down his face, tugging at his short beard.

"Would you have wanted to take a walk once we arrived? You know, maybe grab a few minutes alone to decompress or something?"

He sighs. "I had every intention of parking the truck and taking a long fucking hike into the woods until I found a cliff to jump off of. Why?"

Case smiles at me. "You owe me two hundred bucks."

"Nope," I shake my head. "Hypotheticals don't count. Bet's off."

"You two bet money on how crazy she'd make me?" Lee snarls.

Case nods with an even bigger smile on his face, not

giving a single solitary fuck that he's pissing Lee off more. "Yep, and I won."

"Fuck you guys." Lee turns back to the truck. "Let's get this over with."

I'm shaking my head as I approach the back passenger door, tugging on the handle as the locks disengage. Offering Epi my hand, I lock gazes with the sexiest woman I've ever met. Her effect on me is crazy. Not because she isn't beautiful—because she is—but her attitude does things that make her even hotter in my eyes. "Come with me, Ms. Krushner."

"Where are we going?" She jumps out of the back seat, annoyance dripping off each word. I guess she doesn't enjoy being locked up or left alone.

"We're transferring you to our truck for the rest of the trip."

Staring at me for a minute, she sighs and reaches for her bag. "Fine."

"Leave it," I say as my eyes travel her body and assess her outfit. I was joking about frisking her, but now that I really look at her, I wonder. "How old are your shoes?"

She glances down at the trainers on her feet. "A month, maybe."

"Where did you get them?"

She lights up at my question, and it makes my chest tighten. I like seeing her smile and wouldn't mind making her do that often. "Do you like them? They're limited-edition Balenciaga. They cost a couple thousand, easily."

I stifle the sardonic smile playing at my lips. Women and their shoes, or maybe this is an Epi thing. Yeah, it's probably an Epi thing. "That's great, but *where* did you get them?"

Shrugging, she shakes her head at the apparently ridiculous question. "They were a gift."

"From whom?"

"One of my fans."

"Great." That's all I need to hear. I pick her up and set her back down on the seat, pulling off each shoe and tossing it onto the seat behind her.

"What are you doing?"

"Your shoes are going on a joy ride. If everything checks out, you'll get them back in the morning."

"How am I supposed to walk without my shoes?" She huffs.

I lift her in my arms and carry her back to our truck, feeling both Lee's and Case's eyes on us as I pass them. After setting her down in the backseat, I reach across and snap her seatbelt in place, inhaling her sweet spun sugar scent while I have my nose practically buried in her hair.

Fuck, she smells like candy. I bet she tastes like it, too. "Now, Ms. Krushner. Be a good and cooperative little client for us, and I'll figure out a reward for you later."

Her eyes flash wide as I swing the door closed, drowning out any complaints before she can voice them.

I shout at my partners. "Are we ready or what?"

Case walks to the driver's side with the keys in his hand. "See you in a couple of hours, man."

Lee nods, removing his gun from his back and holstering it under his shoulder. "Have fun."

CASE TAKES THE SCENIC ROUTE, giving Lee time to take the tan van on a wild goose chase, while I spend half my time ensuring we don't have a tail and the other half fielding a million questions from our brat—I mean, client.

"That place we went to earlier, the one downtown—do you all live there? Like full-time?" She's kneeling on the floor with her face cradled in her hands as she leans over the center console, which means she has her back arched and ass is in the air.

Damn, I wish I was in the backseat right now. It would take everything within me not to have my face buried between her legs.

I take another deep breath, trying to will all these filthy thoughts away. Case was right. I'm going to have the worst case of blue balls if I don't knock it off. "Yeah, that's our place."

"Together?"

"Yes."

"Are you straight?" Her head swivels back and forth, gauging both of our reactions, which we keep blank. She continues, "I mean, no shade if you're not. Some of my best friends are gay, but I'm trying to imagine how girlfriends and three men living together works? I mean, it's not like you are college guys sharing a frat house and partying with co-eds."

"Yes, we're straight, and it's not really a problem for us."

"Why not?"

I glance at Case, who is shaking his head so slowly, it's imperceptible to anyone who doesn't know him like I do. This would be a great time to tell her about our lifestyle and give her brain a few days to simmer on it. She'd either be very interested or completely disgusted. Either way, we'd know without ever making a move on her.

Case opens his mouth to speak before I do. "Do you have any dietary restrictions, Ms. Krushner?"

"Call me Epi. Everybody else does."

"Except for your father. He calls you Pip, right?" He raises his brow but keeps his gaze focused on the road in front of us.

That statement seems to rip the chattiness right out of her. She pushes off the center console and sits back in her chair. "Pip is what my mother called me. My father rarely calls me, period."

"Your mother died when you were twelve, right? It must've been hard to be a teenager without a woman around to mentor you." He continues as I turn in my seat to look at her.

She crosses her arms over her chest and stares out the side window, completely ignoring Case's question. "Have you heard from the other team regarding my sister?"

Classic avoidance as a result of unresolved traumas from a young age. Interesting.

I nod. "Yes, we've heard from them. They have a lock

on her location. Hopefully, we will have some good news in a couple of hours."

She sighs and nods, but doesn't look at me.

"We should grab some supplies before we hit the cabin," Case says, interrupting the silence her mood change has brought on. "Is there anything you like or don't like to eat?"

She shakes her head, her voice hollow. "I don't have any dietary restrictions. I try to eat healthily, but I'll pretty much eat anything you give me."

Fuck my brain.

Even with her mood shift, I can't keep my mind out of the gutter, and the idea of her parting her lips for anything I feed her makes more blood rush south. It's amazing I'm still conscious at this point.

"We have canned food and non-perishables at the cabin. I'm sure we can make do for tonight until we can grab fresh produce and other healthy shit in the morning," Case says, oblivious to the thoughts rolling around in my head.

She nods, her expression far away and deep in thought, and then, like a flipped switch, her entire demeanor changes. She lights up, a broad smile spreading over her lips, her eyes bright as she turns and faces me. "Healthy shit? You make it sound so appetizing."

Part of our PsySpecOps training is to analyze behaviors and look for underlying motivators in a person's actions. Epi can turn it on with a snap of a finger, something I'm sure she learned how to do in her childhood out of self-preservation, and I doubt she knows she does it.

"Porter is an excellent cook," Case says, shoving a thumb in my direction.

I smile but say nothing, my eyes taking in every little nuance of her attitude shift.

"Sounds yummy." She licks her lips and locks gazes with me, her eyebrows twitching as she expects a response.

I give her none.

She sticks her bottom lip out and shrugs. "Do you think we'll get there soon? I really have to pee."

"We're about fifteen minutes out. Can you hold it?"

"Yeah," she sighs.

Seventeen minutes later, I've performed a perimeter check of the cabin before going inside and clearing all the rooms. Then, I run outside to throw the switch to the main power at the pole, turning on all the lights before signaling the all-clear to Case.

Epi runs upstairs to use the restroom while Case and I grab our bags and tactical gear, dumping them in the living room.

"Anything from Lee?" I ask Case, who shakes his head.

I pull open a few cabinet doors. "Guess I'll see what there is to eat. He'll be stuck with leftovers, if there are any."

"Worst case, he can eat an MRE." Case shrugs.

"What's an MRE?" Epi bounces down the stairs two at a time. She's a peppy little thing, her body practically vibrating with pent-up energy.

I drag my eyes off her and return to the cans of

rations we brought up last time we were in the area. "It stands for Meal, Ready to Eat. It's the lightweight, portable rations we'd keep on us when on deployment, where there weren't drive-thrus, mess halls, or five-star restaurants."

"They last forever, so we always store them along with our other non-perishables," Case says from my side.

She takes a seat at the island and places her face in her hands. "Were the three of you in the military together, too?"

"Yep." I nod, rifling through the cans, checking expiration dates.

"Wow. So how long have you known each other?"

"Since we joined at eighteen," Case answers.

"And you've been together ever since?"

"Yeah." I place cans of green chilis, canned chicken, cream of chicken soup, spices and rice on the island and then give Case a chin tilt. "We need water."

He nods, running out the door to turn on the pump without saying a word.

I turn on the faucet and wait for the water to run clear.

She purses her lips and motions to the food. "Mmmm. Fancy."

I shrug. "It'll fill our bellies for the night."

"I like being stuffed full."

Her words and teasing tone cause my eyes to snap to hers at the same moment Case walks in from outside. "The water's on."

She stares back at me for several seconds, a battle of

wills as to who will look away first occurring before she breaks eye contact and turns to Case. "Is that why the toilet wouldn't flush?"

"Yeah. We turn the water and electricity off when we aren't here." Case's eyes roam over the ingredients on the island and flashes me a thumbs up before sitting down to sort through one of our tactical bags. All of our weapons are pristine, but I know him. He'll disassemble and clean each one while we are here, just for something to do.

"What do you have in there?" She spins in his direction, crossing one long bare leg over her knee. Every move she makes is part of a tease, and she's damn good at it. So good, I wonder how much of it is intentional and how much of it is subconscious. How much of it is honest-to-god flirting, and how much of it is a survival mechanism—a need to give people exactly what she thinks they want?

Case holds up a nine millimeter handgun—his eyes drinking in every inch of her flesh from her bare toes on up—before arching an eyebrow in her direction. "Things you are not to touch. Have you ever handled a handgun before?"

Her smile turns sickly sweet. "I've handled many big, dangerous things, including handguns."

His jaw tightens, and it's at that moment I know she's gotten under his skin, too. He looks like he's on the edge, and I wonder if he'll leave her with me to take a long hike off a cliff? "Do you turn everything into a sexual innuendo?"

Her back stiffens and her lips part before she snaps them shut. "I've found most men respond favorably to it."

"You mean you've found you can put most men under your thumb quickly by teasing them into believing you want exactly what they want." His gaze once again rakes over her, but this time it's deliberate, and meant to make her uncomfortable if it's not the kind of attention she's looking for. "How many men have offered you their kingdoms in your short time on earth?"

Her lips quirk, as if reflecting on a happy memory. "It doesn't matter. None of them have ever offered what I want."

"What is it you want?"

She shrugs and hops off the stool, her feet on the stairs before she responds. "I'm going to make sure that the toilet is flushed."

We both watch as she ascends the stairs and disappears into the primary bedroom with the en-suite bathroom.

"We're in big trouble," Case says to me, his gaze fixed on the empty stairwell.

"Yeah, she knows exactly what she's doing," I agree.

"She's too young to know what she's doing," he grumbles.

I shrug. "She's twenty-two and has experienced shit that we never will."

"Yeah, that's what I mean." Case turns to me with a frown and goes over to the bank of computer screens attached to the cameras on the property, turning all of them on.

My eyes bounce from the workstation to the stairs, but I keep my voice low. "I've been watching her, reading her, and as soon as shit gets heavy inside her head, she shuts it down and becomes social media Barbie."

"Exactly what the camera is looking for," he completes my thought. "She's been doing it for a long time."

"She'd benefit from some time on the cross with Lee," I muse. "He'd flog all those repressed feelings right out of her sexy ass."

Case chuckles and shakes his head, refocusing his attention on the computer screens, adjusting the images and moving the cameras around to check their functionality. "Just because she's seen a lot, traveling the world and all that shit, it doesn't mean she's experienced much."

"Maybe she's waiting for the right men to give her that experience?" I offer.

He frowns. "How many women do you know who are looking for men versus a man? We are an intense trio in general. In the bedroom is the next level. What we desire isn't exactly mainstream or for the faint of heart."

"She's pretty fucking strong. With us, she wouldn't have to be," I point out, my eyes glued to the landing where she should appear any minute.

"We don't know if that's what she wants."

Now it's my turn to frown because he's got a point, too.

He sighs and stands up from the screens, retaking the seat with the tactical bag splayed open in front of it. "Let's worry about keeping her alive for now. Once this is over, we can worry about the other stuff."

I turn my back to the stairs and my attention to our dinner. "You're right. I know you're right."

ENTES TUERE
PUNIRE IMPIOS

Chapter Six

EPIPHANY

"GOING BACK to my question earlier about your living situation and dating—" I wait until I have both of their attention trained on me "—do you like to share your women?"

I see the flash of surprise on both of their faces, but it's when Porter says *Yes* at the same time that Case says *What?* that I have my actual answer.

Case glares at Porter. "Dude."

Porter shrugs and turns back to the bowl of ingredients. "She's not stupid."

I smile, a satisfied smirk spreading my lips. "Not only is she not stupid, she's actually quite bright. You forget, I have traveled the world many times over. I've been exposed to all kinds of lifestyles, and while I may not have partaken in everything myself, there is very little I'm unaware of."

"It doesn't freak you out?" Case asks.

I flash them a reassuring smile. "Quite the contrary. I

find alternate lifestyles fascinating and have lots of questions. Like, how does it work in reality? How does daily life happen? Do you get jealous of each other? What are the logistics of—" I rotate my hands in the air, my fingers curling and flexing to represent different motions and body parts.

Porter laughs but directs his eyes to the pan filled with our dinner.

Case mutters under his breath, "Lee is going to fucking kill us."

"Is he the boss? Like, in all things? Are the three of you *together* together?"

Porter puts the casserole in the oven and spins around, wiping his hands dry on a towel. "You are getting very personal, Epi. Are you prepared to answer as many questions as you are asking?"

I shrug, "Off the record?"

Case leans back in his chair, slinging his arm over the top. "Everything between us is confidential, sweetheart."

Sweetheart? Why does that make my insides tingle like when Lee called me a good girl earlier? "Sure."

"Asking and answering personal questions could make things around here... uncomfortable, and we don't know how long we are going to be stuck here together." Porter leans his hip against the counter and pins me with his beautiful gray eyes.

I get what they're saying, but I learned a long time ago to live and let live. What people do, as long as they're not harming me or mine, is none of my business. Except, in their case, I'm a nosey little thing and totally want to know everything.

I find it interesting.

And I find these three men fascinating.

All my fantasies from the car ride earlier come roaring to life, a flood of warmth infusing the lower half of my body. I figure the best way to put them at ease is to tell them one of my own stories. "One time, I went to a fashion show in Milan and met this Bollywood producer who invited me to a party on a yacht off the coast of Abu Dhabi. The entire inside cabin was nothing but a giant orgy. There were naked people everywhere, having sex on couches and against the walls. There was even one woman spread out as a buffet on a giant dining room table, and everyone—men and women alike—took a nibble."

"Jesus," Porter mutters.

"How old were you?" Case asks.

"Seventeen, maybe sixteen."

"Did you participate?"

I can hear the genuine concern in Case's voice and realize this story isn't turning him on. It's pissing him off.

I shake my head. "Oh no. As soon as my chaperone and I saw what was going on, she took me to the upper deck. We hung out until the next shuttle boat came by to take me back to my hotel. You see, while I've seen a lot, I was fortunate to be protected and only took part when I wanted to."

"And your father allowed this?" Porter all but growls.

I bite my lip, involuntarily casting my eyes to the

ground. I don't like talking about my parents because I inevitably give away a fraction of my insecurities when I do. "The only thing my father cared about was that I was safe. As long as he didn't have to deal with me—meaning my chaperones kept me out of trouble—he didn't care what we did or where we were. It was an unspoken rule in our family. *Don't let anything happen that gives her father no choice but to deal with her.* Landing in the hospital or jail would've required my father to get involved. For everything else, I had a passport and a credit card."

"And your chaperones? Were they good to you?" The hardness around Case's eyes eases, and maybe I'm imagining it, but it's the concern etched in his features that makes me want to open up to him. To both of them, really. Once again, I need to remember that, like my chaperones, my father paid them to take care of me.

Of course, maybe I'm so desperate to have an actual connection to someone, I'm projecting my feelings onto these hot studs. It doesn't hurt that they are the three Bs— buff, beautiful, and badass.

"My chaperones were mostly females, approximately ten years older than me. They enjoyed the lifestyle our connection afforded them. You've probably heard of a couple of them. One of them dated a famous rap star and made a sex tape. She now has her own *entourage*." I use Case's words from earlier.

Porter leans forward on the island, locking gazes with me. "We don't deal in pop culture, Epi."

My brow furrows. "Did you know who I was before this morning?"

He shakes his head. "No. If we had seen you before, we would've remembered."

His gaze is so intense and penetrating, I need to look away. "Do we have anything to drink?"

"We have bottled water, seltzer water, but that's about it."

"No alcohol?" I wince.

He shakes his head. "We're on duty, but if you want us to pick up something tomorrow, we can do that when we're out."

"That's okay." I nod, even though sadness fills me as I remember my father paid them to protect me. I'm just another job and after this is all over—on a day that I hope is a happy ending for my sister—I will never see these men again.

Our conversations have been too intimate, so I put on my camera-ready face and glance back and forth between them. "How long until the food is ready?"

AFTER DINNER, I sit on one end of the couch with my knees tucked under my chin. I am beyond bored, and I have no idea what to do with myself. I've never gone this long without being connected to something, whether it be my YouTube channel or my Instagram feed or even a good book. Right now, I can't even listen to music. Without my phone, I have nothing to hold my attention.

I want to return to our conversation about their lifestyle. Have they ever shared a girlfriend, or has it just been women they have sex with? How does a woman date three men? Does she see them one at a time, or does she go out with all three of them, but only pay attention to one at a time? They never answered my question about whether they are *together* together.

But unfortunately, all those questions are personal, which means they get to ask personal questions in return, and I'm not ready to answer any of those. "How much longer do you think it will be until Lee gets here with my stuff?"

Case looks up from a gun he's cleaning. "I wouldn't expect to see any of your stuff until morning."

"Morning? Am I supposed to sleep naked?"

They exchange a look but say nothing until Porter finally speaks. "If you're ready for bed, you can have one of our shirts."

Ohhh? I like the idea of sleeping in one of their shirts.

Why is wearing a man's clothes so sexy?

"And my toothbrush? My face cleanser? My silk, hypoallergenic pillowcase?"

Case laughs. "We have new toothbrushes in their packaging in the bathroom. Other than that, I don't know what to tell you."

I huff, wrapping my arms around my stomach, pushing up my breasts. Porter sits across from me at a computer that they informed me is not on the Internet. It's a closed-circuit monitor tied to sixteen cameras spaced around the property. This place has sensors on the road, cameras in the trees and additional triggers in the driveway. There's no way someone is sneaking up on this property without them seeing it. "Have you heard anything about my sister yet?"

Porter glances down at his watch and shakes his head. "Even if Bravo Team-3 got there before sunset, they will wait until after it is dark to extract her. They need time to survey the property and see who comes and goes. Then, depending upon what they find when they go in, they will have to move her to a secure location. We won't hear from them until all that's over, which I suspect won't be for a few more hours."

"Why don't you relax, Epi?" Case sighs. "I know you're twitching without all your gadgets, but the best thing you can do is go to bed and try to get some sleep."

"Where am I supposed to sleep?" I walked through a bedroom upstairs that had an attached bathroom, but I didn't see another bedroom or bed.

"You'll take the primary bedroom upstairs. We'll sleep down here."

"Fine. I guess I'll go to bed. I don't suppose either of you have a sleep aid?"

Case and Porter exchange another look filled with unspoken words. It's kind of annoying how well they know each other, that they can communicate without speaking—especially when it's about you.

Porter stands and goes to his bag, grabs a prescription

pill bottle and pulls out a tablet, breaking it in half. "Do you always require a sleep aid?"

I shrug, trying to come across as nonchalant. "For years I was constantly changing time zones, so I got used to taking something to help me sleep. Now I can't fall asleep without them."

He hands me half a tablet and my bottle of water. "These are formulated for my weight, so we'll start with half."

"Okay." I don't have the heart to tell him that a full-strength tablet probably won't make a dent. I've been taking something to sleep since I was twelve years old to chase away the nightmares. I haven't had a bad dream in years, but the drugs are habit-forming, and I don't want to think about how long I'd have to go without sleep to kick it.

"Do you want a shirt?"

I flash him a little smile. "I thought I'd sleep nude."

Case coughs and brings his eyes up to meet mine. "We'd prefer you didn't, in case we have to make a getaway in the middle of the night."

I frown, jutting my bottom lip. "Party pooper."

I WAKE to a deep voice downstairs. I left the door cracked open, so it takes nothing for me to stand near the opening undetected and listen to what they say.

"You didn't trigger the driveway sensors. I wonder if they are busted?" Porter says.

"I left the truck a half a mile down the road on the edge of the field of view of the southeast camera." That's Lee's voice.

"You're just out of view then, because you didn't trigger that camera sensor either," Porter says.

"We should test all of them tomorrow, just in case," Lee sighs.

"So, nothing?" Case asks, his voice sounds groggy.

"Nope. I drove around looking for that fucking van, and then I took a very obvious drive up and down the flattest and longest dirt road I could find. After sunset, I sat there for two hours. I pulled out all her electronics and let them broadcast for a couple of hours before sticking her phone with everything else back in the box. Then I went through all of her stuff looking for a tracker or something out of the ordinary, finding nothing. I'm not confident about the train case, so I left it behind."

I hear a big thud as something heavy hits the wood floor. "Here are most of her clothes and some of her girl stuff."

Porter laughs. "Girl stuff?"

"Man, I don't know what half of this shit is. It looks like she has six bottles of the same thing." I hear them moving around, but I can't see them. Skulking around in the shadows is so unlike me. This is way more of a Leti move than mine, but I'm hoping to catch a few minutes of uncensored truth.

"What do we have to eat? I'm starving," Lee grumbles.

"There's a bowl of green chili chicken and rice in the microwave for you," Porter says.

"Fantastic." I hear the buttons on the microwave being pushed. "Have we heard from the other team yet?"

"No," Case says, his voice becoming louder, as if he is standing at the base of the stairs and looking up at my door. I hold my breath in response. "But I suspect we will any minute now."

"Where is our client?"

"Upstairs asleep. We gave her a sleep aid. So, I'm hoping she's out cold."

The microwave door opens and closes. "Sleep aide, huh?" I hear Lee say around a big bite of food, his voice muffled.

"Yeah. One of mine," Porter says.

"Yours would be the best ones to give her." There's a full minute of silence, making me itch to open the door and creep down the stairs.

"What aren't you telling me?" Lee says, as an empty bowl and fork clink in the sink.

"Ms. Krushner asks a lot of questions," Case says.

"Yes, I know," Lee grumbles.

"She's smart—instinctual and perceptive," Porter sighs. "Very little escapes her attention."

"And?" Lee's voice is getting deeper, but louder, which I suspect means he's angry. "Spit it the fuck out, man."

"She guessed our living situation, and we didn't deny

it," Case mutters under his breath, so low I barely catch it.

"Worse than that, I confirmed it," Porter adds.

I hear the front door open and three sets of footsteps as they march out of the house without speaking another word. Tiptoeing over to my bedroom window, I peer into the darkness to see if I can catch a glimpse of them. After a couple of seconds, they're standing in a circle twenty or thirty feet from the house, and by the way Lee's arms are flailing, I'm guessing he's not happy.

Which is too bad because I have another million and two questions.

A phone rings downstairs.

Then again.

When none of them make a move to come back to the house, I realize they can't hear it. Wondering if it's my sister, I rush down the stairs and grab what looks like two cell phones glued together to make a thick one.

"Hello?"

Silence greets me at the other end.

"Leti?"

"Identify yourself," a gruff voice barks on the other end.

"This is..." I pause as the door swings open and Lee stares down at me with a murderous glare. He puts his finger against his lip and shakes his head, his other hand out, palm up.

The look on his face scares the hell out of me. I put the phone in his hand and press my lips together.

He lifts it to his ear as Case and Porter enter behind him. "This is Lee."

I can hear the raised voices coming through the other end of the line. Lee's jaw clenches and the muscles in his cheeks flex, but he says nothing as the caller rants on. After a full minute, he says, "Are you done?"

Porter looks at me and shakes his head as if he's disappointed, running his hand over his closely cropped hair. Then I glance at Case, who looks almost as angry as Lee, his cheeks flushed red. I slump down and perch on the second from the bottom stair.

"Repeat that part," Lee says calmly. Thirty seconds later, he says, "Fuck."

I can't take it. If he's getting information about Leti and his only response is to say fuck and not my eye contact with me... well, that can't be good. My body shakes, a chill coursing through my limbs despite the warm air around us. Before I know it, tears are streaming down my cheeks and a sob rips from my throat.

Jeez. I haven't cried in so long, I forgot how to do it.

I cover my face with my hands to shut everything out as my world falls apart and darkness closes in.

"Hold on a second," Lee says, but he sounds like he's underwater, his voice distorted, his words—nonsensical.

Someone pulls me into their lap and wraps their arms around me. It takes a couple of seconds for me to recognize Porter. Case is also there, sitting next to him and pulling my legs up onto his lap. Lee is kneeling in front of us, pulling my hands from my face. His features are much softer now as he searches my face.

"Leti is okay. They got her out without firing a single shot."

"She's okay?" I squeak.

"Yes."

Uncontrollable sobs take over my body. I turn into Porter's chest to hide my face as tears pour out of me. I haven't wept like this since my mother died, and I certainly haven't cried like this in front of other people since before her funeral. My cheeks burn as I cry until I have hiccups and dry tear ducts. When I finally pull my face from Porter's chest, it's soaked between my tears and snot draining out of my nose.

Lovely, Epi.

"I'm sorry." I drag my eyes up to meet his.

He gives me a gentle smile, using his thumb to wipe my cheek. "It's okay. You needed that."

A tissue appears between us and I take it, trying to smile despite the tears and mascara and snot sliding down my face. "I made a mess of your shirt."

"I have more."

I glance at my legs and then at Case, who also gives me a warm half-smile. His hands are large against my calves, which he rubs absentmindedly. Then I turn to look for Lee, who is standing in the kitchen with his hands crossed over his chest. When I notice he's no longer on the phone, panic sets in. "Can't I talk to Leti?"

He nods. "They're getting her settled, but they'll call back in ten minutes."

I let out a deep breath and take an inventory of my body. I need to pull myself together before talking to her and make sure I resemble the sister she's known for the last ten years. If I fall apart on her, it will only freak her out and she's been through more than enough. She deserves better from me.

Patting Porter on the chest, I attempt to pull my legs out of Case's hands. When he flashes me a confused look, I smile. "I need to wash my face before talking to Leti. It'll freak her out if I'm not me. I have to be strong for her."

He sighs and releases me, standing and helping me to my feet.

"I'll be right back." I run up the stairs and turn on the faucet, splashing cold water on my face repeatedly until the phone rings downstairs.

Heavy footsteps alert me to their approach as they climb the stairs, saving me from going back down to face them. Lee stands in the dark doorway, the lights from the living room causing his shadow to glow as he engulfs the opening. He hands me the phone and says softly, "She's okay."

Taking the phone from him, I turn my back and walk to the bed. Perching on the edge, nervous energy causes my hands to shake and my voice to quiver. "Leti?"

ENTES TUERE
PUNIRE IMPIOS

PSYSPECOPS

Chapter Seven

LEE

THE LAST FOUR days have been utter hell. Once, I was trapped in a building during a gunfight for five days with only two MREs and one canteen of water, and that was a fucking picnic compared to a few days with Epiphany Krushner.

I could kill Porter for admitting our sexual preferences and lifestyle choices because that knowledge fuels her attempt to break us.

It's not supposed to be this way.

The brat does not break the Doms.

We tame the brat.

While she gently needled us from the moment we met, the true torture didn't start until after Reese's team secured Leti and the two of them talked on the phone. Since then, she's been relentless.

Whining, teasing, complaining, teasing, arguing, and then more teasing.

How does a woman tease three men, you may ask?

Well, she's special because she not only gives us attention as a group, but she torments us individually, too.

First, if any of us are standing, she brushes up against us, or drops something and then bends over to pick it up.

And her mouth! She turns everything we say into a sexual innuendo.

She's a fount of *that's what she said* jokes.

It's a curse and a talent.

For example, the morning after we arrived, Case took her outside to teach her how to shoot one of our guns. While I have no intentions of her ever putting her hands on one, I relented once he gave me a good argument. Standing in a clearing facing the woods, Case reached around to fix her grip, and she used that opportunity to arch her back and grind her ass against his cock. That sent him on an hour-long hike.

Then, in the middle of the night, we woke to shouts from the downstairs bedroom Porter slept in, where our little brat crawled into his bed in nothing more than a tank top and a pair of boy shorts.

When I asked her what the fuck she was thinking, her response was, "I felt like it."

This morning, she started the day doing yoga in the living room where I was sleeping on the couch. I woke up to a downward-facing dog inches from my nose, and although she has clothes with her, I swear she only wears the shortest of shorts and sports bras.

I'm now on my own hike, checking the cameras stationed along the perimeter of the property and sneaking up on the truck to see if someone's tampered with it. Being cooped up with three other people twenty-four-seven would grate on most people, but I usually have no problem.

Of course, I've never had somebody test my control nonstop either.

I swear, I've taken so many fucking cold showers in the last four days, my cock is raw from jerking off.

You think she'd be scared or in a perpetual state of heightened awareness knowing that although her sister is safe, her would-be kidnappers are still at large. But she seems to be completely immune to this knowledge.

Or at least, that's what she wants us to believe.

Porter mentioned watching her mask slip into place multiple times on the drive, and I've witnessed it a few times myself. She's been burying her feelings for so long she probably doesn't know she's doing it, and I know she's mortified about crying in front of us the other night.

Unfortunately, when Reese's team extricated Leti, there was only one person at the house to take into custody. He's some burnout who did not know why he was there. All he knew was he got paid one thousand dollars to sit on his ass and watch TV for twenty-four hours. He knew somebody was in the back bedroom, but he had no idea who they were or why they were there, and his only job was to call a number should someone come by the house.

He failed the one task he was given. Instead, Reese called the number and the same masked voice we caught on tape at the house answered.

Another regret I have for not going after the tan van.

I walk through the front door at the same time that Porter walks out of the downstairs bathroom, shirtless with a towel around his neck. Thirty seconds later, Case walks in behind me from god knows where. I glance around the room and then take a couple of steps to the left to look up the stairs where the primary bedroom door is wide open.

Listening for movement, I hear nothing. "Where is she?"

"I think she's upstairs," Case says at the same time Porter replies, "I thought she was with you."

"Epi?" I call up. When I get no response, I glance at the monitors, but Porter's already checking the cameras.

He hisses. "Son of a bitch. She's at the truck parked on the road."

I pat my pockets to look for the keys and realize they're empty. "I'm going to string her up and beat her ass until it's purple!"

Case is already running to his truck, his keys in hand. "Come on, let's go."

We jump in the truck and tear ass down the road. I clench my fists on my thigh and imagine the worst punishments possible for her. She thinks going a few days without internet access is torture? She doesn't know the meaning of hell, but she's about to learn.

Case pulls his truck in front of mine before she has the driver's door closed. I'm out of the passenger seat, ripping her door out of her hand before she can close and lock it.

Her wide eyes betray her shock, but she keeps her voice light—and amused, lyrical lilt to her words. "Hey, Lee."

I grab her upper arm and yank her out of the seat. "Are you fucking kidding me right now? Where the fuck do you think you're going?"

She resists and pulls against me as I drag her over to Case's truck. "I am not your prisoner."

I throw her over my shoulder and walk to the driver's side, where Case has the back door open. Tossing her across the seat, I am on top of her before I can think twice about it. Pinning her with my chest, I put my nose to hers and glare down into her eyes. "No, you weren't a prisoner, but when we get back to the house, I'm tying your ass up. Then we can talk about what being held captive feels like."

She seems to understand she's pushed me to my breaking point, but then has to take it one step further by flashing me the tiniest of smirks.

I narrow my eyes. "Are you sure you want to go down this road with me?"

"I'm not afraid of you."

"You should be."

She chuckles darkly. "I'm not afraid of any of you."

The challenge in her tone pisses me off. "You can only poke a caged animal for so long before he bites."

Her smirk turns into a full-blown smile. "Poke, poke, poke."

I hear Case suck in his breath as I lift off her, which

means he also heard her challenge. She sits up and meets both of our eyes with unwavering conviction.

"You have a half mile or two minutes to change your mind and attitude, otherwise—"

"Otherwise what?" She raises her brow.

I glance at Case, his feelings obvious.

There is no otherwise.

There is no going back.

This is going to happen.

"Fuck it. You don't get to change your mind." I slam the door shut.

Three minutes later, I'm walking into the cabin with her slung over my shoulder. She's fighting me, squirming and whining—kicking her legs with her hands bunched around my belt—all of which only makes me harder.

Porter's gray eyes flash, his chest expands, and I hear the unspoken words tumbling out of his mouth. *About fucking time.*

"Grab the Velcro cuffs."

He nods, diving into one of our go bags.

I set her down in front of the banister, grabbing her hands and shoving them so high above her head, she has to stand on her tiptoes. "You choose. Either you strip, which we know you have no problem doing, or we'll strip you."

"I kind of thought you were taking me to the bedroom." Her eyes are wider than earlier as she glances between the three of us.

"Pleasure happens in the bedroom. Punishment happens here." I tilt my head to Porter, who stands above her on the stairs. He criss-crosses the Velcro through the banister and over her wrists until she's secure. "You wanted our attention, Epi? Now you have it."

Case flips open a blade and stands beside me. "You can't volunteer to strip now. I guess we'll cut your top off of you."

Not that she can complain about a ruined shirt. She's wearing one of ours. The little imp has been stealing our clothes—when she wears them—all week.

He takes a step toward her and grabs the hem of the T-shirt.

"Wait!" she says a bit breathlessly. He stops, his eyebrow cocked. "What are we doing?"

I lean forward and put my mouth near her ear. "You've been teasing us since the moment you came bouncing your little ass into the house. You've been waving your shit in our faces, goading and pouting like the little brat you are, for four days. Don't tell me you don't know exactly what you want from us."

She sucks in her breath but says nothing.

I pull back to look her in the eye, letting my gaze trail down her body. Her nipples are hard, poking through her shirt, begging to be plucked and played with. Brushing against the fabric with the crook of my finger, I smile when she shudders. "If you want to deny us, do it now, but know you only get to do it once. Say no. Say this isn't what you want and we'll back off, but then everything ends. The teasing, the pouting, the flirting, the near nakedness and sexual innuendos—all of it stops."

Shaking her head, she meets each of us in the eye to

include Porter as he looms above us. "I don't want to stop."

"Good girl, but you're still going to be punished." I take a step back as Case moves forward, splitting her shirt open right down the middle without a word. She's bare underneath, her breasts perfect mounds with dark pink nipples aching to be sucked.

But not until her ass is warm and red, and her pussy is dripping wet.

"Has someone spanked you before, pet?" I grab her jaw, forcing her to look at me. If she says yes, I might lose it, not that I have a right to be possessive about her past.

Her future is a different conversation.

"Really spanked?" Case says from beside me.

She shakes her head, but I see a flash of defiance in her eyes. Our sweet brat isn't going to back down an inch, and I love her for it.

Reaching behind my head, I pull off my shirt before I unbuckle my belt, sliding it through the loops with a loud smack.

Her eyes widen and lips part. "Oh."

"Don't worry, pet. We won't take a belt to your virgin flesh today, but someday..." I let the threat, promise, sit there.

"Please tell me you have a paddle in your truck." I glance at Case, who is already walking out the door.

"Damn straight I do."

"You want to finish stripping our little brat?" I ask Porter, who flashes me a big grin as his answer.

He walks down the stairs, smacking his palm against

the banister with every step he takes, causing a vibration to reverberate against her back. When he comes around to stand in front of her, he puts his face into the crook of her neck and inhales, groaning against her smooth, fragrant skin. "Are you scared?"

"No." Her breathy response betrays her anxiousness.

I growl. "She told me she wasn't afraid of any of us."

He chuckles with a dark rasp in his tone. "I bet that made you mad."

"It made me something." I unbutton my pants, letting them sag on my hips. The head of my cock pokes out of my boxer briefs, pre-cum beading at the top. A small moan escapes her lips, her eyes bouncing between my cock and my face before returning to Porter, who is sliding his fingertips down the center of her chest and past her navel.

"Should we see if the idea of being spanked makes her wet?" Porter says as he kneels in front of her.

"I'm willing to bet she's soaked and we haven't touched her yet." I smirk.

Case walks into the house with two paddles, one wrapped in leather, the other well-oiled, aged wood. He hands me the wooden one, my favorite, and then yanks off his T-shirt, throwing it next to mine on the couch. There's something different about this moment. While the three of us have taken women together before and played out similar scenes, none of the women we've ever known were like Epiphany.

I'm sure Victor would have a stroke if he knew what we were about to do. I know I would if I was anyone other than one of the three men standing in this room, faced by this woman, right now. But Epi causes me to break my own rules, which is something I never do. Yes, she's been a pain in the ass, but the kind I've enjoyed. Watching her break down that first night, I saw the pent-up pain she carries, and it called to me on a primal level. Porter got to cradle her in his arms, but I wanted to be the one to comfort her. A spike of jealousy I rarely feel cut through me that night, and I had to walk away to stop from growling at him.

She's done many things over the last few days that have warranted this moment, but running out of the house and endangering herself, I can't let that go without serving up some kind of punishment.

I don't know what tomorrow holds for us, but for tonight, she's our little brat and we're set to tame her.

Porter pulls down her athletic leggings and slips off her trainers, tossing them across the room. She's completely bare save for the thinnest landing strip of hair. He smacks her thigh. "Spread your legs."

All of her attention is on him as a rosy color hits her cheeks. Jesus, I wasn't sure this woman could blush considering the way she's been prancing her near-naked ass around for the last week.

When she doesn't readily comply, he pinches her inner thigh, causing her to cry out. "I said, spread your legs."

Need rumbles deep inside of me. While I'm the most dominant of the three of us with the tiniest sadistic streak, there is something about watching Porter so worked up and frustrated that even he's demanding. He's a teddy bear compared to Case and me—the nice guy who loves snuggling and revels in aftercare.

"Is she ready?" I ask as he helps her spread her legs as wide as she can, considering she's on her tiptoes.

He runs a finger over her lower lips and then turns to me with a smile before swirling his tongue over the glistening arousal covering his fingertip. "She's ready."

"Loosen her binds so she can assume the position."

Porter stands up and does the one thing none of us has done. He threads his hands in her hair, pulls her head back and kisses her possessively, deeply, until she's leaning into him, begging and panting for more. "Remember on the drive when I promised you a reward?"

She nods, licking her lips.

"You take your punishment like a good girl, and I'll give you a reward."

Her eyes are wide as I approach her, but then she steels her features and raises her brow. "Now what?"

I grin, completely turned on by her defiance, and trace her cheek with my fingers as Porter loosens her binds. Her arms sag, and she drops a couple inches until she's flat on her feet. "Turn around."

We don't wait for her to do as she's told. Case has his hands on her hips and turns her forcefully until she's facing the banister. He pulls her back roughly so, once again, her ass is nestled against his cock. Hissing in her ear, he bends forward, giving her no choice but to do the same. "Remember this position?"

"Wrap your fingers around the balusters, pet," I say at

the same time as I lift her hands and place them where I want them. Porter adjusts the Velcro and once again secures her wrists.

Case kicks her legs apart, placing his palm flat against the middle of her back. "Just like this. You will stay in this position, your legs apart, your ass in the air, until we're finished with you. Do you understand?"

"Let's hear it, pet," I bark, giving her the lightest tap of my paddle against the plumpest part of her delectable ass.

Her body jerks and her eyes light up as she looks over her shoulder at me. "What do you want me to say?"

"Tell us you understand."

She huffs and rolls her eyes. "I understand."

"Oh—" I take a step back, biting my thumb to stop the slew of profanities on the tip of my tongue.

Case chuckles darkly and fists a handful of her hair, putting his mouth at her ear. "You need to pick a safe word before my brother tears your pretty little ass up."

"I don't need one."

"Everyone needs one," he growls.

"Fine." she huffs. "Cinnamon."

"Cinnamon it is." He presses a hard kiss on her cheek and then stands up, smacking her ass hard with his open palm.

She yelps, but then turns to smile at him as if to say *thanks for the tickle.*

Before he can say something, which I know he's dying to do, I deliver a medium strength blow to her backside, wiping the smile right off her face. Her lips part as if to protest, but then she shakes her head and looks straight ahead where she makes eye contact with Porter, who leans across the stairs with his face an inch from hers through the baluster.

I place my palm over the red mark, rubbing softly and sliding my index finger lightly over her glistening pussy lips. She arches her back, silently asking for more, which makes me smile.

For a pet that hasn't been spanked, she's responding beautifully.

I remove my hand and Case delivers his smack on the alternate ass cheek, following up with the same care. Each time, she winces and her head drops a little more, but she doesn't cry out, or drop to her knees, or call *cinnamon*. We trade off for only a couple smacks each when Porter gives us the sign *that's enough*.

Taking in deep breathes to calm the beast—a desperate need to sink deep into her, mark and claim her as mine, as ours—I take a step back and give him a nod. "Undo her restraints."

ENTES TUERE
PUNIRE IMPIOS

Chapter Eight

EPIPHANY

MY ARMS FALL LOOSE, changing my equilibrium as I tumble to the ground. Except I don't hit the floor. I'm floating weightlessly through the air—my back and knees cradled with the utmost care. I open my eyes to see Lee looking down at me, my cheek resting against his bare chest.

"Is my punishment over?" In my brain I'm saying something snarky like *that didn't hurt*, but that wouldn't exactly be true. It hurt as it went, but my brain disconnected from the pain and embarrassment of having two grown men spank me—and of me liking it. I've seen scenes played out in BDSM dungeons or at fetish parties. As I've stated before, I've witnessed a lot, even if I haven't taken part. I've also seen submissives after they've been spanked or flogged, so I know what it looks like when their brains disconnect from the rest of their bodies.

I've seen their glassy eyes and love-drunk expressions.

I wonder if that's how I look right now?

"Yes, pet. You did good."

"Very good," Case says above my head. It's then I realize he's stroking my hair in a gentle, loving manner.

"How do the backs of your thighs feel when I touch them?" Porter asks from the other end of the couch. He's sitting with my feet on his lap, my knees bent, his hands pressing against my tender flesh.

It's sore, but not unbearable. "It's okay."

"Okay enough to get your reward?" He leans down and kisses the top of my knee.

Lee tilts my chin and claims my mouth, my lips parting in surprise. He doesn't waste any time, plunging his tongue into my mouth to taste me, testing my depths as he explores. Before I can think twice about the situation or how we look to the outside observer, I'm running my fingers through his hair, cupping his head and kissing him back, exploring him as he discovers me.

"That's our girl," Case chuckles behind me. "My turn."

Lee pulls back and Case turns my face to him, kissing me with the same fiery passion Lee and Porter did earlier. I moan into his mouth, my entire body waking up from the momentary slumber I succumbed to from the paddling. His hand slides down my neck to cup my breasts, his finger deftly rolling my nipples back and forth.

Other fingers slide from the back to front and back again along my pussy, spreading my arousal and gently separating my slick folds. I can't pretend to be shy as I let my knees fall open, granting Porter complete access as he slides two fingers inside of me. The invasion makes me gasp, my pussy walls clamping down on him as if I've been on the edge of orgasming for days. I suppose I have been with all the teasing, flirting, and fantasizing I've done.

These men, my security detail, my bodyguards, have certainly given me a lot of fodder to work with as I lay in bed alone each night.

"Fuck, sweetheart. You are tight," Porter hisses, placing a kiss on top of my hooded clit.

"Let me see." Case releases my breast and slides his hand over my belly, curling his fingers as he slips them inside of me. He pumps them in and out a few times before bringing them into his mouth. "She tastes good, too."

"It's time for your reward." Lee grins and Porter dives face first between my thighs, pushing them apart with his broad shoulders. He latches onto my clit, sucking the tight little bundle of nerves up against his teeth, before lapping with a hard press of the tip of his tongue in tiny circles.

My head drops back, my mouth falls open as I stare into Lee's gentle eyes. I had no idea Lee had a gentle anything. He certainly hasn't looked at me once since the moment we met with anything other than a hard, shrewd, calculating, and condemning gaze.

But this is different.

This is so much more.

"That's it, pet. Disconnect your brain and feel the

pleasure we want to give you. Doesn't Porter's mouth feel good between your legs?"

"Yes." I bring my hand up and cup the back of Case's head as he sucks on my breasts.

"And doesn't Case's mouth feel good on your tits?"

"Oh, yes."

"Two men feasting on your body. Should I nibble on your lips? Then you'll have all three of your men devouring you."

"My men," I moan, the pressure between my legs building fast because of Porter's skilled tongue.

"That's right. Your men." Lee bends down and claims me in another possessive kiss, stealing my breath and swallowing my screams as my orgasm crests over the edge. I come hard, my body trembling in their arms.

Without a spoken word, I'm lifted off of Lee's lap, away from Case's mouth, to straddle Porter's thick thighs. He kisses me hard, my taste and scent all over his trim beard and full lips.

"Don't you taste like candy?" he murmurs against my lips.

You know? I kind of do.

Rustling of clothes, boots landing with hard thuds to the left and right of me, makes me look over my shoulder as both Lee and Case shed what is left of their clothing. All three men are breathtaking, with thick, corded muscle and smooth skin with patches of coarse, dark hair in all the right places. But it's their erections that cause me to take in a calming breath. They are large, thick, swollen, and dare I say, very intent on me.

Lee growls and wraps his big hand around his cock, stroking himself slowly. "Do you like what you see?"

I bring my eyes up to his, remembering my bratty tease on the drive up here. It seems he too remembers if the slight curve of his lips is any sign. Not one to back down, I lick my lips and nod. "Very much."

Case chuckles darkly, and I'm learning to recognize the difference between this and his regular laugh. This one promises pain or pleasure, or maybe for Case they are the same. "A true brat—back-talking any time she isn't out of her mind with pleasure."

"I guess we'll have to keep her enthralled," Lee says.

"Or her mouth full." Case grabs his cock, sliding up and down his length in a mesmerizing rhythm.

"Who do you want to fuck your tasty little pussy first, Epi?" Porter's mouth hovers over my ear, his breath tickling my neck.

"What?" I turn to him.

"Whose cock do you want to stretch your tight cunt first?" He pokes me through his shorts. Of the four of us, he's the only one with a stitch of clothing left on. It doesn't matter. With a gentle roll of his hips, I know he's just as well-endowed as his partners, and so it's like he's asking me to choose between my three favorite designers.

I glance over my shoulder at both Lee and Case. "I can't choose."

Lee offers me his hand. "Come here."

Crawling off Porter's lap, I stand and take his hand. He pulls me against his hard body, wrapping one arm around my waist. His widespread palm slides over my ass, my skin stinging from his touch. One finger slides gently between my ass cheeks, and he rubs a small circle over the hole. "Have you ever been taken here?"

My eyes shoot wide as I shake my head emphatically.

He grins. "Don't worry. We're not going to take you there tonight."

Breathing out a sigh of relief—because honestly, I'm already worried about them hurting the part of me that has had a penis in it, much less that virgin entrance—I relax into his embrace.

He tilts his head to the couch, to where Case now sits with his knees splayed wide, his cock hard and ready. "On your knees, pet. Case is going to keep your sassy mouth busy for a bit while I take you from behind."

I look up at him, a driving need to talk back on the tip of my tongue. Not for calling me pet. To be honest, I kind of like that and all the other nicknames they give me. But calling me sassy feels like a challenge I need to rise to.

His grin widens, and he fists a handful of my hair, driving me to my knees. "You just can't help yourself, can you?"

I'm face to face, eye to eye with Case's penis, the head reddish purple and weeping with pre-cum. I glance up and he raises an eyebrow, as if he's waiting for me to say something to provoke him. Instead, I smile before licking him from base to tip, letting the clear drop fall from my tongue to land on my bottom lip before sucking both into my mouth.

Case smiles. "Good girl."

Something warms inside of me, and I guess I really do like being called that. I run my hands up his thick thighs, wrapping one around the base, the fingers on my other hand digging into his hip. Taking him deep, I swallow him whole, gagging before sliding him out of my mouth.

"Careful now. We can work you up to deep throat." I nod, taking him back in as deep as I can.

Lee's breath is on my ass as he slides his finger along my wet slit. "I've got to have a taste," he says, placing his palms on my tender flesh. He spreads my ass cheeks wide, his tongue thrusting into my pussy, rimming the tight opening where his cock will soon be. As he flexes his fingers, a sharp sting of pain mixed with indelible pleasure shoots up my back, making me moan around Case's erection.

I pull back, but Case threads his fingers through my hair and cups the back of my head, holding me in place as he brings his hips up and thrusts deep down my throat. "Fuck, your mouth is exquisite."

Tears fall down my cheeks as Case fucks my mouth, but it's the overload of sensation that has me unsure of how to feel. Lee's tongue plunging in and out of me, circling my asshole and then plunging deep within me again feels amazing yet filthy, but I like it too much to feel bad about it. I'm desperate to have him fill me, and if I could bark out a demand to him, I would.

Porter kneels beside me and puts his mouth near my ear. "You're doing so good, baby. I love watching you swallow Case's cock. Are you going to gobble up his cum, too?"

"Fuck, she does taste like candy," Lee says, his big hands wrapping around my waist. He presses the head of his cock against my sex, pushing and pulling in tiny pulses as if to tease me. "This is going to be a chore... she's so tight."

"Get it done, man." Porter places a kiss and then a nip on the back of my neck before moving underneath me, pulling my nipple into his mouth. "She needs it."

Lee pushes his hips forward, burying his cock so deep into my pussy, his thighs smack my ass. I gasp and then whimper, bringing my eyes up to Case's. He grimaces and flexes his fingers against my scalp, a possessive growl in his tone. "Keep going."

I have two men filling me, both growling as they move slow and then fast and then slow again, keeping me full and on the edge.

I'm close.

I'm so fucking close, and I just need a bit more to send me over the edge. Balling up my fist, I smack Case's hip and cry out, "More."

Lee's hips stop, his voice incredulous. "Did she just smack you?"

Case's fingers tighten, and he yanks me off his cock. I gasp for air, my nipple popping out of Porter's mouth, and look through blurry eyes to focus on Case's face. I can't tell if he's angry or disappointed, but at this exact moment, I don't care—not when I'm so close.

"Listen up, brat. You don't come until we say you can."

"Please," I moan. At this point, I'm willing to beg. I've never been backed off the edge like this before, and I don't like it.

"Are you begging or demanding?" Case narrows his eyes.

"Begging," I whine, trying to keep the sharpness out of my tone.

"Do it better."

I stick out my bottom lip, my voice quivering with pent-up need. "Please make me come."

Case's eyes go over my head to connect with Lee's, who slides his cock in and out of me at an excruciatingly slow pace.

Oh my god, this is torture.

I want more.

I want faster.

I want harder.

"Get back to work, pet," Lee says from behind me, his thumb circling and pressing against my asshole.

I swirl my tongue around the head of Case's cock and then swallow him down. I notice the faster and harder I suck on him, the faster and harder Lee's strokes come. Within a minute, I'm panting, once again on the edge, ready to spill over.

"Fuck!" Lee shouts, his fingers digging into my hips as I explode into a million tiny pieces.

At the same, Case pulls me off and fists his cock, jerking himself to completion. "Open up."

I do as he says without complaint, opening my mouth and sticking my tongue out as he shoots hot cum down my throat.

Lee pulls out of me, shooting his load all over my back at the same time. I went from being double stuffed to empty in seconds, and all I really want is more.

Porter's underneath me, pinching, plucking, and biting my breasts and nipples, his ministrations gaining my focus as my pussy pulsates the last of my orgasm and come drips down my inner thigh.

Lee reaches over and grabs one of their discarded T-shirts, wiping my back clean before wrapping his arms around my waist and picking me up off the ground. Porter is standing up and shucking off his shorts, his cock just as long and thick as his partners.

He sits down and puts his arms out, a sweet yet devilish grin on his face. "Give her to me, you fucking savages."

Lee chuckles, placing me on Porter's lap so that my knees straddle his thighs.

Porter runs his fingertips reverently over my breasts, causing me to look down.

All over my chest are red to purple bruises forming. "Oh, my god."

Case hisses. "Fuck man, what did you do?"

Porter squeezes my breasts together, flicking his thumb over my sore extended nipples without apology. "You leave your mark one way. I like to leave my mark in other ways." He shifts his hips and lifts my ass. "Ride my cock, baby."

He enters me smoothly, my ample arousal coating my lips and inner walls. "Ah, fuck, your pussy is so good."

"Oh," I toss my head back and run my hands up his muscular biceps, wrapping my fingers around his neck as I roll my hips back and forth. "So good."

ENTES TUERE
PUNIRE IMPIOS

I TAKE the washcloth Lee hands me and clean myself up, watching as Epi bounces up and down on Porter's cock. Then I see the flash in Lee's eyes as he takes in the dozen or more hickeys decorating her chest.

"Fuck," he hisses under his breath.

Exactly what I was thinking. Yes, we marked her ass, but that is easy to hide under a pair of pants. Her chest? One slip off a shoulder or dip of her neckline and someone—especially someone like us—will notice. We're not supposed to mark, kiss, spank, or fuck the client—I'm pretty sure I read that somewhere when I signed on with the company—and we've done all of that and more in a couple of hours.

But Epiphany is idyllic for us. From her beautiful face, perfect curves, and sassy fucking mouth—she is pure perfection. She also took her punishment like a queen—our queen—and I can't wait to claim her as ours.

Lee told her we wouldn't take her ass tonight, and

that's fine by me. We wouldn't do it while hundreds of miles away from home anyway, but last we heard, Epi's would-be kidnappers are off the grid and even Soren can't find them. While he's doing the technical stuff from the secure location where they are protecting Leti, Victor, along with a couple of guns for hire—two ex-PsySpecOps operators who live down in Tennessee—are hunting known associates of Claudine Humphrey. Last time we talked to Soren, he felt like he was getting close, but we still don't know how much longer we're going to be here.

Not that fucking Epi nonstop will be a burden or anything. I think I can handle the task, but can she handle the three of us for a week?

A month?

A lifetime?

I stand behind Porter sitting on the couch and smile down at Epi when she opens her eyes. She licks her lips and puts her hands out to me, beckoning me forward. Leaning over Porter and shoving his head aside, I cup her neck and kiss her with a sweetness I rarely display during the daylight hours. I cuddle occasionally, but only in the darkest hours of the night when not even my lover can see my face or read my thoughts. Yet, with this little brat, our perfect Epi, I can't stop myself from showing her a bit of gentle love. "You want to come again, sweetheart?"

She whimpers and nods her head.

"Lean back." I slide my hand down and press my middle finger against her clit, letting her ride my finger at the same time she rides Porter's cock.

"Oh, fuck yeah," Porter groans, and I'm guessing her

inner walls have clamped down on him as her climax builds to its crescendo.

He grips her hips and works her faster, chasing his own release when Epi cries out, her eyes closed tight. Watching her come makes me hard and achy to be inside of her.

And it is my goddamn turn.

Porter lifts her up and pulls out just as he comes, shooting long, thick pearly ropes onto his stomach.

Picking her up off of his lap, I cradle her in my arms and walk over to the single wingback chair. I sit down and rest her on my lap. She immediately curls in, like a cat seeking warmth, so I stroke her thigh gently, soothing her as she nuzzles her face into my neck.

"How do you feel?"

"Boneless."

Slipping my fingers between her legs, I gently stroke her pussy lips. "Are you sore?"

"Not right now, but I'm thinking I will be later."

"I can run you a bath."

Her eyes are closed, and yet she smiles at me. "I thought Porter was the nice one?"

I brush the hair back from her face and place a gentle kiss on her lips. "He is—" I lower my voice so not even she can hear me. "—but I'm the one that falls the hardest."

She opens her eyes and looks at me. Shit, maybe she heard me? I think she's about to say something when she smiles and says, "Are you going to fuck me now?"

"I want to, but I'm willing to wait until you have more energy."

"You like it when I'm bratty, don't you?"

"It gets me hard."

She wiggles in my lap. "You seem hard right now."

"Sweetheart, I've been hard since the minute I first saw you."

She kisses my nose and whispers, "I like you, too."

"What are we doing over here?" Lee takes a seat on the ottoman next to us. He reaches out and strokes her hair, gathering it up and playing with the ends.

She turns her head and smiles at him. "We're taking a break."

Porter kneels on the other side of the chair. He grabs her foot and massages it, starting at the arch and moving towards her toes.

She moans, her eyes fluttering shut.

"She has pretty toes," Porter mumbles.

I let my gaze trail down her long legs and nod in agreement.

"She's got a pretty pussy, too," Lee says, bringing a handful of her hair to his nose and inhaling deeply.

"I'm the only one who hasn't had my face buried between your legs yet. I feel like I'm missing out."

"Oh brother, you're definitely missing out."

"Maybe we should lay her out like a buffet, so I can feast."

Lee cracks a smile and nods. "I couldn't agree more." He stands up and moves the ottoman over, patting the plump cushion.

I'm completely on board with this thought process,

picking her up and laying her down lengthwise on the footstool.

She smiles up at me. "Do you want me to say something bratty now?"

I smile back at her. "Hit me with your best shot."

Her smile grows wider, and then she says in her whiny voice, "I'm bored. Entertain me."

"Fucking brat," I chuckle. "Lay your head back. Take Lee's cock as I eat you out. Show him how good your mouth can be when you're not talking back."

Her eyes narrow and I think she's going to mouth off, but then she complies. Seems the best way to needle Epi is to call her a brat.

Good to know.

Easy to do.

I lift one of her legs and run kisses up her thigh, inhaling her sweet scent. My brothers haven't come inside her, not that it would stop me if they had. I've tasted myself and them before. We all have. It's part of sharing a woman, and although I'm not swooping in to suck up their leftovers on the regular, I don't let the runoff shy me away from getting a woman off.

Of course, we don't make a habit of coming inside our women for multiple obvious and not so obvious reasons. Coming inside her goes hand in hand with taking her sweet ass, both of which I hope we will do sooner rather than later.

She's the one for us; I'm sure of it. But once this is over and we go back to our regularly scheduled lives, will she want us? Can someone with a public-facing persona be in a relationship with three men?

Especially men like us?

Coming inside of her—regardless of the birth control situation, which we didn't bother to ask about—is about marking and claiming her, something we intend on doing only once in our lives. When we play at the club, we always glove up.

Since we are on the job, none of us thought about bringing condoms—not that I want anything between her and me, if I can help it.

Her clit is plump—engorged from the attention we've shown her tonight—and sensitive, which is just how I like it. I flick my tongue across it, and she shudders, moaning and reaching down with one hand to stroke my hair. I glance up and see Lee bouncing his cock against her lips before sliding into her open mouth. She's stroking him with her other hand, and I have to admire her ability to multitask.

I suck her clit and lick until I'm stroking inside her with my tongue, lapping up all the sweet juice that over-flows from her pussy. She's been wet since before we stripped her down, her cunt gushing when she comes. "Porter and Lee are right. You taste like candy."

I curve my fingers, slipping them inside to stroke her g-spot.

"Fuck," Lee hisses, throwing his head back. "I like it when your mouth is full, pet."

As soon as I have her dripping wet with her pussy quivering around my fingers, I stand up, lean over her and shove my cock deep inside without warning. Her cunt grabs hold and milks me, her climax instantaneous. I pump my hips, chasing my own release through her tight grasp, while Lee looks like he's close to coming himself.

I hook my forearm under her knee and spread her wide, sliding in and out of her slick heat until I can no longer hold back. Pulling out of her, I shoot my load onto her stomach, painting her with my cum. Lee quickly follows, pulling out of her mouth and coming onto her chest.

A washcloth flies in from my side and smacks me in the face—payback from Porter for pushing his head out of the way earlier. I slide him a bit of side-eye and pick up the washcloth, wiping Epi clean.

Lee staggers back to sit on the couch while I lean over Epi and kiss her with all the possessiveness I feel coursing through my veins. "Such a good girl."

She wraps her arms around my neck and pulls me down on top of her. "I like it when you call me good."

"And when I call you a brat?"

"I like that, too."

Porter smacks me on the shoulder. "Why don't you take a shower, and I'll make us dinner?"

"Do you want your men to bathe you, or do you need some time alone?"

"Has anything about me made you think I want to be left alone?"

"No, not really."

I stand up with her legs wrapped around my waist,

her arms looped around my neck, her body glued to my chest, and tilt my head towards Lee. "Shower?"

As if answering for him, the phone rings. We exchange a look, because there's only two people who would call this number. I dip my chin, giving him the answer to the silent question in his brow, and carry her upstairs to the bathroom.

"IS THIS CRAZY?" Epi asks once we are holding each other under the warm spray.

"Is what crazy, sweetheart?"

"What we did downstairs?" She gently uses her teeth and bites the cleft in my chin.

"Not to us." I kiss her forehead and then grab the soap, lathering up my hands before rubbing them over her gorgeous body. "Are you okay with what happened downstairs?"

"Yes," she whispers.

"Are you sure?" I drop to one knee and lather up each thigh, touching her gently between her legs, and looking up at her with heartfelt sincerity, but in my head I'm screaming—*please don't regret this.*

Smiling down at me, she nods. "I'm wondering when we can do it again?"

"Ah, that's my bratty girl." I let the water rinse us clean, then I spin her around and put my mouth to her ear. "Brace yourself against the wall."

Epi puts her hands out in front of her and I line up my cock, slipping inside her warmth. "Oh, fuck. You feel amazing, sweetheart."

She moans, tossing her head and arching her back, offering her pussy to me, begging me to plunge deeper. I wrap my hands around her waist and pump my hips, taking her hard and fast until her cunt tightens, and she comes for me again. "Oh, Case!"

I'm depleted.

Hard, but depleted, so I continue to pump my hips until she sags underneath me, and then I pull out and spin her around to face me, claiming her lips in a punishing kiss.

I have so much I want to say, but can't right now.

This isn't a one-time thing for us, Epi. You need to know that.

We want this.

We want you.

Not just once, but for a lifetime.

Is it too soon to say all that?

Abso-fucking-lutely.

And so instead I say nothing. Besides, this isn't my conversation to have alone, and this isn't the type of conversation you have after one night.

She sags against me, breathless, but sated.

I let out a content sigh and grab the shampoo bottle, lathering her hair and massaging her scalp until she is barely conscious, her arms wrapped loosely around my waist, her head resting against my chest.

This... This I could do night after night for the rest of my life.

After washing her hair and body, I wrap her in a couple of towels and leave her on the bed with a kiss on her forehead. "Come downstairs when you're ready."

I run down and throw on a set of clean clothes before walking outside to find Lee and Porter talking over the grill. "Who was on the phone?"

"Soren. He got a ping off the tracker in the hub. It was within two miles of here."

The blood drains from my face. How fucking stupid are we to allow ourselves to get carried away, risking our client's life, the woman I'm sure we all love, to get off while on the job? "When did it pop hot?"

Lee shakes his head. "Came on about three hours ago and they've narrowed down a fifty-mile radius over that time. It comes on for a few minutes and then goes off for twenty."

"Three hours?" I look across the woods and over the brush toward our parked truck on the road.

"Exactly what I was thinking," Lee says. "Did she activate something? Bring something back into the cabin with her?"

"We locked her electronics in the lead-lined box." I can't think of what would have changed over the last few hours, unless she had a tracker implanted in her vagina and we knocked it loose.

"Fuck." Porter tosses down the grill tongs and runs inside, returning with her designer trainers. "She brought these back with her from the truck."

He tosses one to me, the other to Lee. I find a tiny glued seam in the heel's tread and flip open my knife, cutting a big hole in the sole. With no finesse, I rip it apart until a tiny tracker falls onto the deck floor.

"Son of a bitch!" Lee picks up the chip and glances around the property. "We should move her."

"We should hide her and lure these fuckers in. I'm tired of this shit," Porter growls.

Lee and I exchange a look, but it's the sound of a large vehicle out on the road that has me running into the cabin to check the monitors.

Tan van. Motherfuckers.

"It's them!" I'm pulling my boots on at the same time as Lee straps on his weapons.

Grabbing my tactical bag and truck keys, I yell at Porter while running after Lee out the door. "She's upstairs. Get her secure. We'll be right back."

We tear ass down the dirt driveway and swing to the left onto the road in the direction the van was traveling per the monitors. "They are not getting away this time."

Lee slides the hammer back on his Glock, putting one in the chamber. "Let's hope they aren't a diversion."

ENTES TUERE
PUNIRE IMPIOS

Chapter Ten

EPIPHANY

"WHAT'S GOING ON?" I bounce down the stairs with a new type of energy invigorating each step, my hands busy plaiting my damp hair. Seconds ago, I was ready to pass out. Now, I want to be touched, licked, kissed, and played with by my men.

I'm addicted.

I already can't get enough.

Case proved that to me in the shower.

Porter looks up from the monitors and holds his hand out to me. "Come here, baby."

I think he's going to pull me into his arms and kiss me some more—which is really all I want to do for the foreseeable future—but he doesn't. Case told me what we did was normal and right, but I'm sure if I took time to think about what we just did, I'd find something wrong with it —or with me.

Fortunately, I feel so good right now, flying high on

endorphins with no desire to come down, that I don't care.

He guides me to the chair and points at the monitors. "Watch these and tell me what you see."

I shake my head. "What's going on?"

"The tan van's back, the one following us the first night, and we found a tracker in your trainers."

All the feel-good endorphins drain out of me as I glue my eyes on the monitors. I can't believe this is happening. I can't believe Claudine is so obsessed that she'll risk jail time or death.

Well, I guess she can't avoid prison—that bridge has already been crossed.

"Are we in danger?" I glance over at Porter as he straps weapons on to his body.

"Don't know, Epi. But I won't let anything happen to you." He looks up from what he is doing. "Is there anything on the monitors?"

"No. Nothing."

He walks out front with a plate and comes back with charred meat, tossing it on the island. Then he shuts and locks the front door, before dropping metal shutters over the kitchen window. "Keep your eyes on the monitors, especially the ones in the upper right corner. If you see any movement, yell."

Then he walks into the back bedroom, the sound of shutters dropping there, before he climbs the stairs and protects the window upstairs. I turn around to watch him as he walks back down the stairs.

He shakes his head. "Eyes on the monitor, baby. Not on me."

"There's nothing happening."

"Good." He leans down and kisses my temple. "Are you hungry?"

"I was, but not so much now." I look up at him through my lashes.

He takes my hand and pulls me out of the seat, spinning me out and then pulling me down onto his lap after he takes my chair. I wrap my arms around his neck at the same time as he puts one hand between my thighs. His eyes travel over my chest before fixing on the monitors. "I'm sorry I did that to you. I shouldn't have marked you like that."

I glance down at the myriad of bruises decorating my skin. I was overly stimulated with Lee behind me while pleasuring Case with my mouth and hadn't realized Porter was sucking small hickeys all over my chest. "It's okay. I'm a whiz with cover up."

"Still." He presses another kiss against my temple but doesn't look me in the eye this time. "I had no right to mark you as mine."

"You didn't?" Why is he saying this? Does he not want me after this is over?

The phone rings and Porter touches the comm piece in his ear. "Yeah."

I can hear Lee's deep tone, but I can't make out what he is saying.

"I locked everything down, but I'll see you when you pull up." He nods and pushes some buttons on the keyboard, changing the view of some cameras before hanging up. "Roger."

"What's going on?"

Porter's eyes narrow on one camera, but when he speaks his tone is nonchalant—almost blasé—which reminds me that these men, who just gave me the most intense pleasure of my life, are hardened soldiers who have done things I can't even imagine.

Yes, I'm in the public eye, but my fan base is very specific and not violent.

Generally.

Porter speaks as if he is doing something mundane, like editing a video and pointing out all the lighting problems, and not facing a life and death situation. "They ran the van off the road. Two guys fled on foot, both armed. Claudine was in the van and is now in our custody. They have to wait for the sheriff's department to arrive before they can leave the scene."

"The men are armed? Are Lee and Case okay?"

He brings his eyes up and flashes me a small smile. "They're fine. One guy is down, but the other is loose, so I need you to help me watch for any movement near the house."

I stare at the bank of monitors. It's dusk, which plays havoc with images, so at first, I'm not sure if I'm seeing what I think I'm actually seeing. "What is that?"

Porter presses some buttons on the keyboard and zeroes in on what is clearly a man with a rifle. He pushes me off his lap and takes my hand, a gun appearing in his other. "I need you to do something for me."

He walks me back to the wall under the stairs where they had me tethered only a few hours ago. Kicking a section, a hidden panel pops open to reveal a crawl space. "I need you to get in there. Keep quiet and wait for me to come get you."

"But—"

"No buts, Epi. Do as you are told." He secures the door behind me and then I hear him talking on the phone.

"Yeah, he's twenty feet from the front door, southwest corner."

...

"I have her secured."

...

"What the fuck do you mean, stand down? I'm going outside to pop this fucker in the head."

...

"You won't make it in time."

...

"Dammit, Lee. I don't want this guy to get away. He was ballsy enough to approach the house, so he's not going to stop. Let's finish this and be done."

Let's finish this and be done? The desperation in Porter's voice coupled with his apology for *marking me when I wasn't his to mark* really bothers me.

Is he desperate to get away from me?

Now that they've gotten off, and the moment has faded into the next real world crisis, are they over me?

Do they all feel that way?

Case said this was normal, but he didn't mention what comes after this. None of them did.

I press my back against the wall of this small enclosure and take a deep breath, remembering all the times I would hide from my father and sister and the duplicitous mourners in the first few weeks after our mother died. I didn't know how to deal with her loss and often sought solace in self-imposed exile.

Maybe after this is over, I should put myself into a timeout away from the public eye and my legion of fans. At the moment, I can't imagine smiling on camera and shutting all of this away. Could five days away from my followers really have changed me so much that I no longer want to live on camera?

A deafening shot rings out, too loud to not be from inside the house, and I can't stop myself from screaming and kicking open the door. I scramble out of my hiding space and jump to my feet, prepared to fight for my life and the lives of the men I've unwittingly fallen in love with.

Porter is standing with his gun drawn and trained on a man laying across the threshold. He growls as he kicks away his weapon. "Dammit, Epi, I said to wait for me to come get you."

"Bitch!" the man on the ground moans.

I steal a glance at the man's face as he writhes in pain on the front porch. "Brad?"

Porter is cussing under his breath. "Get behind me. Do you know this guy?"

"We went out a couple times, but then he ghosted

me. Why are you trying to kill me?" I lurch forward to get in his face.

"You're such a cock tease. Nothing but a bratty, spoiled bitch. I can't fucking stand you."

Then Porter does something he hasn't done yet—he yells at me with a bark so deep, it cuts and burns. "Epi! Get into the back fucking bedroom so I can secure this guy!"

The viciousness of Porter's anger makes me jump, and I can't help but do exactly what he says, scurrying backwards and then turning to run into the back bedroom with tears in my eyes.

He continues to cuss, and I hear Brad howl in pain. *"Turn around and show me your hands or I'll shoot you in the thigh, and I promise it will be high up and life-threatening."*

I hear the telltale sound of zip ties. Plastic slides against plastic locks.

Brad groans one more time and then a minute later, Porter is standing in the bedroom doorway, his mouth set in a disappointed grimace, his gray eyes fixed on me. "Are you completely unable to do as you are told?"

"I..." I open and close my mouth like a fish out of water, incapable of answering his question, and cast my eyes to my hands in my lap.

I know I'm a pain in the ass, but I don't mean to be. Well, that's not exactly true. Sometimes I mean to be.

The last four days I've been as irksome as possible, but for good reason, to keep their delicious attention trained on me.

That's going to end soon, and I suppose that's a good thing. Right?

It will mean my life is once again mine. I can get back in front of the camera, interact with my fans and travel far and wide to exotic locations, fabulous parties, etc.

Obviously, I can't date. I knew my taste in men was questionable, but Jesus. This is next level bad picker!

I can't believe Brad teamed up with Claudine to kidnap and kill me. What did I do that was so bad to make two people who I thought were part of my inner circle hate me so much?

The phone rings, but Porter doesn't flinch, his gaze taking in every inch of me as if he's dissecting each part of me. Well, I don't like being dissected. I've spent most of my life not letting people get close enough to figure me out, and I will not let a couple of amazing orgasms ruin a perfectly constructed and bedazzled exterior.

"Like what you see?" I smile and cross one leg over the other.

He doesn't smile back. Instead, he answers the phone while glowering down at me. "What?"

...

"Yeah, you heard a gunshot. That was me shooting the second and hopefully last guy. He's bleeding on the porch, but he'll be fine."

...

"She's also fine. Are those sirens I hear?"

...

"Yeah, send an ambulance this way."

AFTER MANY HOURS of tense silence from the three men who were recently deep inside of me, coupled with the hectic activity of the sheriff and EMTs, Lee puts me on the phone with my father. Even though it's close to ten pm, it's not appropriate to sleep another night in this cabin. I mean, one guy is dead, Brad is maimed, and Claudine is on her way to prison. My sister Leti is on her way back to our father's house, so it would be weird if I didn't show up tonight, too.

Porter hasn't spoken a word to me since shooting Brad, and there are all these unspoken things between the four of us. But what do I expect? We were caught up in fear and adrenaline—and maybe boredom—hiding out while others hunted down my would-be kidnappers. What happened between the four of us—what did it really mean?

I'm a woman. Of course, my heart is attached to my vagina.

Of course, my brain is going to interpret their gentle touches as loving.

Of course, I was going to fall more and more in love with every orgasm they coaxed out of me.

But they are men. Big, testosterone-laden men who like to share bratty women. They probably do this all the time. However, I feel confident I'm the only client they've ever done this with. I can tell the potential repercussions of fucking me while under their care are weighing on their minds.

Sitting in the backseat as we make the three-hour trek back to my father's house, I remove my T-shirt and open up my makeup case, pulling out a foundation brush and my best concealer.

I catch Lee's eyes in the rearview mirror. "Don't worry, I'm not teasing you. I thought I'd work a little coverup magic before we get to the house."

"Probably a good idea," he says. "Those will take at least four days to clear up."

"Yeah, I know. I'll keep them off camera, and honestly, after checking in with my father tonight, I probably won't see him again for a few months."

"After everything your family went through over the last week, don't you think things will change?"

I dab dot after dot after dot across my chest, looking like a kid with calamine lotion covered chicken pox. "Maybe Leti and I will spend some time together. Reconnect."

"That would be good, Epiphany. She's your twin. I bet you have more in common than either of you think."

I shrug. "Maybe."

"I'm sure your fans miss you," he says in a voice I don't recognize.

"Maybe." I shrug again because what does that really mean? They miss me? They miss my ten-minute makeup tutorials? Or my five-minute red carpet stories? They miss having me as one of their many distractions as they scroll through their phones for hours on end?

The truth is, after five days most of them have already replaced me. No doubt a rumor started when I didn't come back online as scheduled about me eloping, or being eaten by sharks, or being sold by some drug cartel—honestly, anything and everything is on the table. The internet is a weird place, and they can turn the tiniest blip of fodder into an almost verifiable story.

I'm a little shocked to not be excited about going back to my fans. Who would I be if not for Epiphany Krushner, the person behind Krush Kosmetics and Krush Kruisers?

"Do you have any regrets?" Lee throws the question out there as we enter my father's neighborhood, but his eyes are on the road.

"About?" I know what he means, but like the brat I am, I'm going to make him spell it out. Honestly, I'm hurting right now. We didn't have time to talk or cuddle afterwards. We didn't lay everything out on the table, and now the moment is over. It was no better than a drunken party night where things got a little crazy, but were also easily forgotten in the daylight hours.

"We crossed a line back there, Epi. We shouldn't have—"

"It sounds like you're the one with regrets." I slip my T-shirt on over my head and sit back on the leather seat with my arms folded across my chest.

His eyes come up to meet mine in the rearview, and then he flips on the cabin lights so that we can clearly see each other. "Listen to me, pet. I don't have one fucking regret. Not one. Whatever repercussions come from this, it was worth it. You were worth it."

My heart melts at his words. "Is that how Case and Porter feel?"

He says nothing for a minute as he negotiates the security gate on my father's property. He pulls around to the front of the house and puts the vehicle in park. "I can't speak for them, but—" he turns around in his seat and hands me a business card "—if you want to ask them, here's our information."

Before I can look at the card, my father's assistant swings my door open—Walter standing a few feet behind him. "You're home."

"I am." I quickly glance at Lee, who cusses under his breath before opening his door.

He pops open the trunk and takes out my bags. My father pulls me into a bear hug. "I'm so glad this is over and both of my daughters are home." He lets me go and quickly clasps on to Lee's hand. "Thank you for taking care of her."

Lee looks at me and then meets my father's eye. "Yes, sir."

Yes, sir? That's all he has to say?

Clearing his throat, Lee hands my bags over to my father's assistant. "I'm sure Victor will be by in the morning to check on everyone, but if you need me directly—"

"Oh, no, no, no. I wouldn't dream of bothering you without going through your boss. And yes, Victor and I have a ten a.m. scheduled for tomorrow."

"Okay." Lee rubs the back of his neck, looking the least confident I've ever seen him. The man is a cocky rock with a rock-hard cock, so this discomfort is off-putting. "If there is nothing else, I'll head home."

My father wraps his arm around my shoulder, pulling me tight against his chest. "Yes, thank you so much."

Lee's name is on the tip of my tongue, but honestly, I'm too shocked to know what to say. Do I call out his name, run into his arms, and kiss him in front of everyone? I'm frozen in place, indecision leaving me a body with no brain as I watch him drive away.

Finally, I turn to my father. "Where's Leti?"

"She's in her room, Pip."

"Okay. I'm going to go check on her." I lean in to kiss him, and he wraps me in another bear hug.

"I love you, daughter. I know I don't say it often enough, and I know I've been a shitty father, but I have always loved my girls."

Something inside me breaks, and I melt into his embrace, wrapping my arms around his waist. "I love you, too, Dad."

We stand there for a solid minute before he finally lets me go. I glance up to find him wiping away a tear from his cheek. "How about dinner tomorrow night? Just you, me, and Leti. Me and my girls."

"Okay." I say, a tad choked up by the emotion rolling off my father.

"Great." He kisses my forehead. "Go check on your sister."

ENTES TUERE
PUNIRE IMPIOS

Chapter Eleven

LEE

I GET HOME after dropping Epiphany off and go straight to my room. Neither Case nor Porter is hanging out downstairs, and I'm betting it is because, like me, they need time to process the last twenty-four hours.

The situation with Epi is complicated, but my feelings about her are not.

I want her.

I want her in my bed.

I want her at my home.

I want her in my life.

I meant what I said to her in the truck. We crossed a line. That never should have happened with a client while on a mission, but we wouldn't have met her any other way.

So, damn the consequences.

But if she hadn't been a client, then the night would have progressed differently. We would have cleaned up, ate, talked, and then fucked into the early morning hours.

The three of us are insatiable, and it takes one hell of a woman to keep up with us, but I'm sure she can do it.

I don't know what happened while Case and I were in pursuit of Claudine and her henchmen, but it was something big because I've never seen Porter so angry. He wouldn't speak to her, would barely look at her, which is why I couldn't assure her that my partners felt the same way I do. I have no idea what's going on in his head, but if he's changed his mind about her, then it's serious enough for me to at least hear him out.

I sense a fight or two on the horizon in this household over the next couple of days. After meeting and then graduating training together, we stopped for a two-day layover in Amsterdam while flying back from our first assignment. That night, after much alcohol, we shared our first woman and discovered we liked everything about the experience. There was no jealousy between us. We complimented each other's strengths and eviscerated any weaknesses.

And the woman liked it, too.

After that night, we sought more shared experiences and had fewer solo ones. A few years ago, we started talking about *the one*. The perfect female who would complete our family.

I think we've found her, and six hours ago, I would have said Case and Porter agreed.

Now?

If something changed Porter's mind, will it also change mine? If not, am I willing to break our pact and pursue her on my own, with or without them? I can't imagine breaking up our family or our friendship, but I also think Epi would be worth it.

There's a knock on my door at the same time I exit the shower. I'm bone-weary from the last couple of days. I never sleep well while out on a mission—even one as easy as hanging out in the woods with a beautiful woman —and I'm ready for bed. "Come in."

Case walks in with Porter behind him. "How'd the drive home go?"

Sliding my hand down my face, I scratch at my beard, which is too long and scraggly for my liking. "Quiet mostly."

"Think we'll be looking for new jobs tomorrow?" Case asks.

I shrug. "Maybe."

He sits on the edge of my bed and sighs. "Fuck it. It was worth it."

Looking at Porter, I ask, "And you? Was it worth it to you?"

"That depends." He crosses his arms over his chest.

"On what?"

"Do we get the girl in the end?"

I drop my towel and slide on a pair of flannel pajama pants. "Don't know. She left the truck hurt and confused. I left frustrated, but at least I told her how I feel before driving away."

"How we feel," Case pushes.

I shake my head. "How I feel. With the mood Porter was in when we got to the house, I have no idea what's going on in your head."

"She scared the shit out of me, man. I couldn't secure the guy because she was jumping in his face." Porter stands up straight and rubs the top of his head as he paces a four-foot section in and out of my bedroom. "I enjoy a challenge just as much as you do, and I have no problem with her giving us shit when we're playing, but when she endangered me and herself, I snapped."

"You yelled at her..." Case says, and I'm betting he's already heard this story and is prompting Porter to tell me everything.

Porter glances between us, the anguish he's feeling palpable. "You should have seen the look on her face. I was so angry, and she was devastated, and I guess it broke me a little. I couldn't talk to her afterwards. I could barely look at her."

"She noticed." I plop down on my bed, stacking my pillows behind me.

"What do we do next?" Case turns to me. "We agree? She's the one."

I shrug. "She's the one I want."

"Me too."

Porter nods, "Me three."

Yawning, I stretch my arms over my head. "I gave her our card. She can contact us in any of a half-dozen ways. I say we give her a couple of days to think about what she wants."

Porter stretches and yawns as well. "If she doesn't call?"

I rearrange my pillows—punching them until they lay just as I like. "Then I guess she'll get kidnapped for real."

"That's what I'm talking about." Case stands and smacks the doorframe as he walks out of my room.

I hope it doesn't come to that. It would make life a lot easier if she made this decision on her own.

NINE DAYS LATER, not only has she not contacted us, but I'm being hauled into Victor's office in the middle of the workday. Not that we have any actual work to do. I've been pinging him constantly, looking for something that's entailed getting my team out of town. Being home and not having contact with her is driving us insane, and we've almost come to blows a few times over the stupidest shit.

Out of coffee? Fight.

Dishes left in the sink? Fight.

Sitting on the couch in a sweat-stained shirt after a workout? Fight.

I walk into Victor's office, surprised to find Reese standing there at parade rest. "What's going on?"

"Close the door." Victor looks up from his computer.

I close the door and also stand at parade rest, twelve years of military training kicking in without a second thought.

"Sit the fuck down. We're not in the military anymore, and I'm not your commanding officer."

Reese and I exchange a look and take our seats.

Victor clasps his hands and places them on his desk,

his shrewd gaze dissecting us both. After sixty seconds of saying nothing, he sighs and leans back in his chair. "Did you know they designed the PsySpecOps training program to create an elite team of super soldiers? Instead of using chemical enhancements like the comic books and movies, the US Army decided the best way to create the perfect man was to take the strengths from multiple men to minimize any weaknesses and, since infusing all of that into one person was deemed impossible, units were designed and trained. It took decades, but eventually they found the best combinations came in threes, and when the program went live, they created teams. The science behind the tests to match up the three is solid, and the success rate of any team graduating after passing the first round together is ninety-three percent."

I glance at Reese, completely confused why we're getting a history lesson we all learned at AIT.

He keeps his gaze forward, but the narrow squint of his eyes tells me he's thinking the same thing.

Victor keeps going. "An unpublished side effect of creating these teams is the participants found they coexisted so well together that seeking relationships outside of their trifecta proved impossible. As straight or hetero-flexible males, finding one woman who is amenable to their lifestyle is difficult at best. Impossible at worst. It's very common for men in our career field to seek their gratification somewhere like a sex club—which is why you all have company provided memberships—where alternative lifestyles and non-judgmental playtime are more common."

"Uh," I open my mouth to interject. This conversation is quickly going somewhere I don't want to go. Women think men engage in locker room talk freely, but the truth is, what goes on with my dick and the dicks of my partners is our own goddamn business. Although, considering he has me and Reese here, I'm certainly curious about the goings-on of the dick sitting beside me.

Victor holds his hand up and shakes his head. "I don't want to hear it. I don't want to fucking hear a word from either of you. I don't know what happened, and I don't want to know. Got me?"

He clears his throat, laying his clenched fists on top of his desk. "The two of you have been up my ass since we closed the Krushner twins' case, asking for an assignment that takes your team somewhere, anywhere other than here. Well, gentlemen, I have nothing for you. And so, I'm sending your teams on sabbatical. I don't give a fuck where you go; I don't care what you do—although, I suggest you spend the time fucking your brains out, so when you come back to work, your heads are on straight."

His eyes bounce back and forth between us. "Understood?"

"Yeah," we grumble at the same time.

"Great. Dismissed."

Reese and I walk out of his office and down the hallway in silence. Right before we split off into our individual team rooms, I stop and blow out a big breath. "Have you been to the club lately?"

Reese also stops, but he doesn't look at me. "No, although we're going this weekend with a guest."

"A guest?"

"A special guest." He turns to face me. "If she shows up."

"No shit? Good on you."

"Don't come to the club this weekend." Reese narrows his eyes. "Just in case."

I chuckle. "Roger that."

"What about you?"

Shrugging, I glance through the window at Case and Porter sitting at their desks with their feet kicked up. "I was hoping she'd come to us, but now, I don't know."

"She's been radio silent?"

"Completely. And she hasn't restarted any of her online presence either. No YouTube, Instagram, or TikTok... none of them."

"Sounds like she's working through some shit."

"Maybe."

"I didn't spend any time with her, but she certainly struck me as a brat. Maybe she expects to be chased?"

"Yeah, maybe."

"Whatever you do, be careful." Reese bumps me on the shoulder with his fist. "See you in two weeks."

I walk into the office and close the door behind me, filling Case and Porter in before presenting them with my idea of how we are going to claim our happily ever after—because it's time.

ENTES TUERE
PUNIRE IMPIOS

Chapter Twelve

EPIPHANY

IT'S BEEN nine days since Lee dropped me off at the house. Leti and I have spent a lot of time together, reconnecting and sharing stories about our lives. Embarrassingly, she knows way more about me than I know about her because she follows me online.

I had to explain to her how what she saw and what really happened wasn't always the same thing.

I'm not surprised by how sheltered Leti's life has been, but I feel horrible about how lonely she was over the years. Our paths took such different directions, and we dealt with the loss of our mother in completely different ways.

But the past is the past.

All we can do now is forge a relationship for the future—something we are both eager to do.

Our father wasn't kidding about grabbing some father-daughter time. We've had dinner five times in the last nine days, which is two more times than we have in the last three years. We've had some interesting heart-to-heart conversations, and although it's too late to save our childhoods, I think we can establish some healthy boundaries as adults as we let each other into our lives.

I haven't heard from Lee, Case, or Porter, but to be fair, I haven't reached out to them either. I honestly didn't think I'd have to. I've never chased after someone before. Part of me wants to drive down to their abandoned building in the middle of their industrial neighborhood and shoot paintballs at the monochrome structure, just to piss them off.

The other part wants to do something crazy to get myself in trouble, so they have to come rescue me.

I can't believe they haven't called.

I grab the mail as I walk into the main house to meet my sister for an afternoon of lunch and shopping. Amongst the myriad of junk mail is a sleek black envelope with silver trim addressed to Leti. I find her in the kitchen drinking a cup of coffee.

"You've got mail." I hand her the envelope, super curious about the glamorous contents.

She frowns and opens it, her cheeks turning rosy as her gaze skims down the card stock.

"Is it a party invite?" I grab my cup of coffee and sit across from her.

Folding the card and sliding it back into the envelope, she bites her lip and looks at me. "You've been all around the world. Can I ask you a crazy question?"

"Of course." I reach across the table and rub the top of her hand. "You can ask me anything."

"No judgment?"

I laugh. "Absolutely judgment free zone here."

She chews on her lip, her eyes bouncing around the room. "Have you ever heard of a woman dating more than one man?"

"Sure."

"No, I mean, dating them at the same time. Like together."

"How many men?"

"Let's say three."

My mind goes instantly to Lee, Case, and Porter. "It's not common, but not unheard of either. Some people call it a reverse harem, some people call it polyamory. What they call it really depends on the group's dynamics in and out of the bedroom. Why?"

Her eyes go back down to the sleek black invitation. "Promise you won't tell anyone?"

I squeeze her hand. "You're my sister. Your confidence is mine to keep and vice versa."

"Something happened with Reese, Caiden, and Soren," she blurts, her cheeks turning a shade of fire engine red.

Temporarily shocked, I stare at her with wide eyes. "What?"

She shakes her head and drops her gaze to her lap. "Nevermind."

Tightening my grip, I pull her hand across the table so she has no choice but to look me in the eye. "Did you want something to happen with them?"

"Yes." A stray tear falls from her eye. "I know it's wrong, and I know I'm weird, but I think I love them."

I can't help it. Joy fills my heart and a matching tear falls down my cheek, dripping onto our clasped hands. "It's not wrong, and you're not weird, and I completely understand because something happened with Lee, Case, and Porter."

Her eyes grow as wide as dinner plates. "What?"

I giggle uncontrollably and motion to the black envelope. "Is that a note from them?"

She glances down and smiles. "They want me to meet them on Saturday night."

"Go." I nod encouragingly.

"How can I?"

"Oh, Leti. I've been all around the world and have met all kinds of people, and the one thing I can tell you is happiness is fleeting, but finding someone to love you the way you want to be loved is special—a once-in-a-lifetime style special. If you found three men who want to love you, whom you also love—well, you've hit the jackpot, and you can't turn your back on it, regardless of what is considered a societal norm."

"What about your men? Have you heard from them?"

I give her a sad smile and shake my head. "No, not yet."

"Do you want to, Pip?"

My smile widens and I do something new. I'm truthful, honest, and vulnerable with my sister. "Yes, but I'm afraid. What if they don't want me?"

"Of course they want you. You're amazing and vivacious and maybe a bit of a handful."

Chuckling, I smile. "I think they like that last part the most."

Leti hops off her stool. Then she lifts her hand up to show me how it shakes. "Look at me, I'm so nervous. I don't think I can do this."

I can't let her back down and lose her chance at love and happiness. "I tell you what. If you go on this date with them, I'll track down my men and let them know how I feel. We'll both be putting ourselves out there, supporting each other while we do one of the scariest things in our lives."

"Yeah?" Her eyes well up with tears again, which makes mine fill up as well.

"Yeah." I hop off my stool and spread my arms wide, welcoming her embrace. "Now, let's go shopping and buy you an amazing dress for your date."

IT'S Saturday evening and I've spent the last two days reassuring Leti this is the right choice for her, although I'm not sure if this is the right choice for me.

What if Lee, Case, or Porter changed their minds about me?

What if they've already found another woman to warm their beds?

What if they decided I'm too much of a brat to deal with?

Well, no matter how this evening goes, I'm prepared to have fun. After I put Leti in a town car dressed in the sexiest dress we could find, I twist my hair up into a high ponytail and climb into my Range Rover, following the navigation to the address on the card Lee gave me. I've driven past this building a dozen times in the last ten days, and it's impenetrable unless they open the garage for food delivery, which I would say they do at least every other day. I'm guessing that with three hungry men in the house, none of them know when one orders food and, therefore, as long as the delivery is food, they'll open the door.

At least that's what I'm banking on as I leave my car in a parking garage downtown and Uber to their address. I wait for the pizza delivery guy to drive up and ring the bell on the outside of the building. When the garage door opens, I sneak in behind him and duck behind their SUV, dropping my bag full of party tricks to the ground. Inside, I have a plethora of ammunition to fire in their direction, including water balloons, glitter cannons, and silly string.

It will hurt if they don't want me, but at least they'll be cleaning the memory of me away for months to come.

Case and Lee come down the elevator looking as delicious as ever in jogging pants and black tank tops. "Who are you?" Lee barks.

The pizza guy jumps and glances behind him, and then back in their direction. "I'm from Dino's."

Case shakes his head. "We didn't order any pizza, man."

The poor driver looks down at the box. "I have an extra large beef stick for Lee, an extra large stuffed for Case, and an extra large salami for Porter."

It takes everything within me not to giggle. I paid Dino's extra to use phony pizza names.

Lee and Case exchange a look and then turn back to the delivery guy. "Show us the pizzas."

He presents them with regular pizzas: one combination, one veggie, and one Margherita.

"Who paid for this?" Case takes the pizzas from the guy, who is getting more nervous by the second.

"I don't know, man. I'm just a delivery driver." He backs away now that his hands are free. "Can I go? The tip's already covered."

"Yeah, man. Have a nice night." Lee glances around the garage, and damn them, they are too smart for their own good.

Case places the pizzas on a tool bench near the elevator door, freeing his hands.

There's no time to waste.

"Surprise!" I scream and toss a couple of water balloons at them from my haven behind their vehicle. One smacks Lee in the chest while the other lands at Case's feet.

"What the fuck?" Case pauses long enough for me to fire two more water balloons, one smacking him in the stomach, the other exploding on the ground between them. Then I grab the glitter cannon and run at them, salting the air with fine hot pink glitter.

It takes approximately two-seconds for recognition to morph into surprise in their eyes. "Epi?"

"That's me." I sing.

Lee's cheeks turn red. "Are you fucking crazy? We are heavily armed men. You know this."

I stop for a second and throw him a quizzical eyebrow. "Are you armed right now?"

They exchange glances, and I know the answer is no. That's why I did this via a food delivery—to catch them off guard.

I might be crazy, but I'm not stupid.

"What are you doing here?" Case shakes his head.

I yank two cans of silly string out of my cargo pockets and aim at them. "Since you never called, I figured I'd drop by and tell you what I think about that."

Then I douse them with silly string, dropping the cans and turning to run when I hear the garage door closing behind me. I'm far enough inside the building that I might not make it safely outside without some home plate sliding action, but I have no choice but to try.

Lee growls as I run for the door. "Grab her!"

I skid to a stop when Porter steps out from behind a pillar, the garage door slamming shut as if it sped up by a factor of ten. "Hello, baby."

Smiling, I glance behind me as Case approaches at more of a stalk versus a jog. "Hi, Porter."

I run back toward Case, dodging him at the last minute and sliding to my knees behind the SUV where my bag of tricks remains. I have three more water balloons, one more glitter cannon, and two more cans of silly string.

Crouching down, I look under the car to find two sets of boots approaching me from either side. But where is the third?

"God, we fucking missed you." Lee pulls me into a bear hug, pinning my arms to my chest. My back sticks to his soaking wet chest as I struggle in his grasp, kicking and thrashing with half my power. Not so much to hurt him, or think I really want him to let me go, but enough to make it interesting. The more I fight, the harder he squeezes, and the wetter my pussy gets. Within seconds, Case and Porter are on either side of me, grabbing one leg to render me pinned.

"You missed me?" I ask, sagging in their arms.

"Every fucking day," Case says.

"Then why didn't you come get me?" I jut my bottom lip.

Porter chuckles as Lee grumbles behind me, the vibration from his chest tickling my back. "Because we had to know you missed us, too."

Case and Porter let my legs down, and then I'm lifted into Lee's arms like a bride. The three men walk me to the elevator, where Case grabs the pizzas off the bench. "Where are we going?"

"You came here to tell us what you think. Well, we have some things to tell you, too."

The elevator doors open and we walk in. Porter leans in and kisses my ear, sucking my earlobe between his teeth. "And we plan to tell you all night into the early morning, baby."

"Yeah," Case says, a slice of pizza stuffed into his mouth. "You're pretty hardheaded, so we think we'll have to tell you again and again and again, until you get it through your pretty little skull."

"What's that?" I grin, an overwhelming sense of relief and gratitude infusing my bones.

This worked.

They let me in.

They wanted me with them.

All of them.

Lee leans down and kisses me on the lips. "That you are ours—now and forever."

The elevator opens up on what I think is the fourth floor. Lee sets me down and then strips off his tank top, leaving the hot pink glitter mess behind on the floor.

Case then hands Porter the pizza boxes and, with a wedge of crust between his teeth, also takes off his wet, glittery tank top.

"You couldn't ring the doorbell like a normal person, could you?" Lee grumbles, wiping at the pink glitter coating his skin.

"What would be the fun of that?" I raise a challenging eyebrow, taking several steps backward, prepared to be chased some more if necessary.

I wouldn't mind being chased.

"You know glitter is going to be a bitch to clean up." Case wipes the tops of his boots with his discarded shirt.

I smile big. "I know. Why do you think I got the extra fine stuff?"

Porter is at my back, wrapping his arms around me, his mouth once again near my ear. "Baby, you are begging for a spanking."

"You think so?" I bat my eyelashes over my shoulder.

"She's begging for a lot more than a spanking," Lee growls.

"Like what?" I flash a taunting smile.

"Like my cock down your throat." Case returns my smile, kicking off his boots and sliding down his joggers to show me he is hard and ready.

I suck in my breath, my mouth watering for a taste of him.

"Now, wait a minute, man. Put the beast away." Porter chuckles, turning me in his arms. "There's a conversation we need to have first. Last time, we played before we had time to talk, and it left us with a bunch of unresolved feelings and unanswered questions. This time, we talk first, and then we play."

There is something about Porter's gray eyes that makes me melt. I sag into his arms and rest my head against his shoulder. "Okay."

He lifts me and carries me over to the sofa, sitting down with me nestled in his lap. Case, with his pants on, sits next to Porter and pulls my legs onto his. He unlaces my boots, pulling one and then the other off, dumping them behind the couch with a heavy thud.

"Why are you undressing her before we talk?" Porter looks at Case.

Case flashes me a big smile. "Saving time, man. At the end of this conversation, we're going to be on the same page. Aren't we, sweetheart?"

I mimic his head bob and smile back at him.

Lee sits on the coffee table in front of me, his elbows resting on his knees. "First things first. How's the last week and a half been? How's your sister?"

Chuckling, I look between the three of them. "You are kind of bringing down the mood."

Case pulls my socks off and massages my feet. "Did you think after your stunt downstairs we'd bring you up here, throw you down, and fuck the brattiness right out of you?"

"Kind of." I say with a slight whine of petulance.

Porter growls in my ear. "Oh, that's coming. Your pretty, soon-to-be bright red ass can bet on it."

Oh god, my pussy clenches at the thought.

Lee puts his finger under my chin and brings my face back around to him. "We've noticed you haven't been online."

I sigh, melting against Porter's chest. I might as well get comfortable because it seems like I have no choice but to get real with them. "I'm reevaluating my empire. Obviously, as the face of Krush Kosmetics and Krush Kruisers Athletics, I have to do some marketing, but after this experience I've realized that not everyone loves me."

"The important people do." Porter kisses my cheek.

I smile, my heart skipping a beat. Did he just tell me he loves me?

I brush it off for now and continue. "Things at home

have been great. My sister is amazing, and I never realized how much I missed her. She's on the verge of being genuinely happy, and honestly, she's the reason I'm here."

Lee's lips curl, as if he knows what I'm talking about. "What happened at the cabin—"

"Yes?"

"There's something you need to know about men like us."

"Okay?"

"We are very disciplined," Lee says.

"We are very controlled," Case adds.

"So, when the four of us—"

"Fucked like wild rabbits?" I flash Lee the sweetest smile I have in my arsenal, the one dripping with snark.

"Oh..." He shakes his head and growls. "You are so asking for it."

"Yes! I am."

Porter squeezes me against his chest. "We wouldn't have crossed that line for a million anyones, but we did for you."

Lee leans forward and hooks my ponytail elastic, pulling my hair free so that it spills over my shoulders. I've noticed he likes to play with my hair, where Case has a thing for my legs and feet, and obviously, Porter likes my breasts, neck, and ears. Between the three of them, my body, mind, and heart are spoken for. "Because we want you. Not just for tonight or the weekend, but for a lifetime. The question is, can you see yourself in a relationship like ours?"

ENTES TUERE
PUNIRE IMPIOS

Chapter Thirteen

PORTER

EPI SMILES and looks each of us in the eye. "Why do you think I've delayed getting back online? I don't know how this would work, but I was hoping to talk to you and figure it out."

I press my face into her neck, inhaling deeply. She smells like heaven, tastes like a candy shop, and I'm desperate to move from the negotiation to the execution phase of this conversation. I've been fucking my hand for two weeks, thoughts of shoving my face between her thighs keeping me perpetually hard. "Be sure, baby. Because once we claim you, we have no intention of letting you go."

"Claim me?"

Lee trails a finger over her breasts, flicking her nipple until it tightens into a hard little bud. Then he rolls it between his thumb and forefinger, pinching it until she gasps. "Remember how I told you we wouldn't take your ass at the cabin?"

Her eyes grow wide. "Yes."

"Tonight, we will."

Her body stiffens, so I nip at her earlobe until she relaxes into my arms. "Don't worry, baby. You'll be so fucking out of your mind, you'll be begging us to do it."

"But you're all so big."

Case chuckles. "We'll fit, and you will love it."

"And if I run away?" There's a challenge to her tone, her eyebrow raised, which snags our attention.

"Then we'll catch you," I say.

"And punish you," Lee agrees.

"Maybe we should give her a head start right now?" Case flashes her an evil grin.

"She still has a punishment coming." Lee pinches her nipple hard. "Don't think we've forgotten about the pink glitter."

She squeals, pulling her knees up under her chin.

Lee looks me in the eye and grins. "Fuck it."

He lifts her out of my lap and walks up the stairs before Case and I can scramble to our feet.

Case sucks in his breath next to me as we walk to the stairs. "Thank god."

"Glad we found a woman bratty enough to throw water balloons and pink glitter at us?"

"Ecstatic."

"She's going to be a handful," I grin.

"Every day for the rest of our lives, if we're lucky." Case takes the stairs two at a time.

When we reach the doorway to the fourth bedroom, the one we furnished specifically for her, Lee has her spread out on the bed with her shirt off. He's pulling off her pants and glances over at us. "It's about fucking time you got up here."

"Are we starting with punishment or pleasure?" Case says, his hands on the waistband of his joggers.

"Pleasure. I can't wait to slip back inside her slick, hot body."

Case crawls onto the bed, immediately claiming her mouth. "Been dreaming about your taste for two weeks."

"He's not lying, pet," Lee growls.

I pull my shirt over my head and kick off my shoes as I approach the other side of the bed. Kneeling on the edge, I smile down at her as Case moves down her body, her eyes already glassy. "Hey, baby."

"Hi."

"I see all the little hickeys I gave you are gone." She sighs as I trace my fingertips over the top of her chest. I push her breasts up, kissing and sucking the soft skin underneath. "I think I'll give you a new one right here."

Epi slides her hand into my hair, drawing me close, while Case moves down her body, settling himself between her splayed legs.

"Fuck," he hisses as he gets another taste of her. "Like cotton candy."

"I know," I murmur, alternating between placing kisses against her breasts—sucking and leaving little love bites behind—and claiming her mouth, plunging my tongue deep between her lips, mimicking what Case is doing to her below. She loves all of it, moaning and writhing underneath our ministrations.

"You want my cock, baby?" I ask as I pull back to sit up on my knees.

Her eyes grow wide and she licks her lips. "Please."

"Open up."

When she does, I slide my cock past her lips, closing my eyes as her wet, hot heat envelopes my sensitive flesh. "Oh, baby, you feel good."

She grips me tightly, moaning her pleasure as Case brings her to the edge. I can tell she's close to climaxing by the way she jerks and sucks greedily at my cock. Her mouth is heaven—my dreams pale comparisons to the real thing—and it takes no time to bring me to the edge of release.

"Fuck." I grip her hair and thrust my hips faster as I come, opening my eyes to find Lee kneeling on the bed on the other side of her, his hands roaming over her breasts, pinching and plucking at her nipples as she slides her hand up and down his length. Next to him on the mattress is a bottle of lube and a dildo about half the size of us, perfect for prepping her.

Epi swallows my cum seconds before she cries out, her lips parting as she fists my cock and rides out her own orgasm, overflowing and soaking Case's mouth. He drinks until she's bucking her hips, and then comes up from between her legs, wiping his mouth and grinning like a loon. "Damn, I love how you come, sweetheart. You're like a gusher candy."

Lee climbs off the bed.

Case changes places with him and lays parallel with Epi. He cups her face and kisses her, mixing her arousal with any trace of my cum left on her tongue. Kissing her breathlessly, he rolls onto his back and brings her with him. Lee helps by bringing her leg over to straddle him.

Once she's laying on top of Case, Lee smacks her ass hard, leaving a red handprint. "On your knees, pet."

Case releases her as she sits up, glancing over her shoulder. "Are you going to spank me more?"

"No." He shows her the dildo. "Porter's going to prep you with this while Case fucks you."

Her eyes grow wide. "With that thing?"

I chuckle. "Baby, that's half the size of us."

"Ride Case's cock, pet, and relax." Lee places his hand on her back and pushes her down so her chest presses against Case's.

I climb off the bed to stand behind her. Squeezing the bottle of lube, I drizzle a fine line over the crack of her ass, letting it slide down as Case grabs her ass cheeks and spreads her wide for his cock. I rub my thumb over her puckered hole in tight little circles until she visibly relaxes, arching her back and pressing her ass into my hand as Case slides in and out of her at a torturously slow pace. Pouring another few drops of lube onto her ass crack, I change from my thumb to my middle finger, pressing and prodding until I push my first knuckle in— sliding in and out until my finger is sucked in tight. I thought Lee planned to take her virgin ass, but considering he gave me the dildo, it looks like I will get those honors. He wouldn't have me prepping her if he didn't want me to go first.

Case, being the first inside of her tonight, will obviously be the first one to mark her with his seed, another first Lee won't get. Part of me wonders why he's willing to give either of those to us, when I know being first speaks to his primal nature. But then, I remember who I'm dealing with, and he's probably more concerned about being gentle her first time, which I am the most prone to be out of all of us.

Pulling my finger out of her ass, I'm pleased when she wordlessly arches her back as if to ask for more. Lubing the dildo, I press the tip against her hole and push forward slowly; the gasp leaving her mouth my first indication she's tensing up.

The groan from Case's lips, my second.

"Relax, pet," Lee says, stroking her hair back from her face and tilting her chin up to claim her lips. She whimpers as he steals her breath away. Case's fingers dig into her hips as I slowly push and pull the silicone dildo in and out of her ass inch by inch. This dildo is five inches long, three inches shorter than any of us, and only half the girth. But as we suspect, she loves it—the tension in her shoulder blades loosening as she grows used to the foreign sensation.

"Do you like it, baby?" I lean forward and kiss her ass cheek, biting the plumpest part of her lithe body.

"Mmhmmm," she moans. "I think I do."

"Are you excited about taking all three of your men at the same time?" I grin, locking eyes with Lee, who waits for her answer.

My heart is full and I'm so thankful this is happening —we are here, now, together—that I feel like a kid on

Christmas. A very naughty, X-rated Christmas, but excited nonetheless.

"Yes," she gasps as Case brings his hips up hard, penetrating deep.

"Are you scared?" Lee asks.

"No." She shakes her head and presses her forehead to Case's. "I'm too stimulated to be scared."

"We're going to take care of you, baby. We're going to make you feel so good." She's no longer tensing, taking Case and the dildo effortlessly, which means she's ready for more.

She's ready for all we want to give her.

ENTES TUERE
PUNIRE IMPIOS

Chapter Fourteen

EPIPHANY

"WE HAVE one more thing to talk about, pet," Lee says as he gathers my hair in his hand.

I crane my neck to look at him, thrusting my breasts into Case's face. "What?"

I'm overloaded with sensations at the moment. Between Case taking me much slower than I would like and Porter working magic on my back entrance in a way I never would've dreamed of wanting—but do—I'm not really in the mood to talk. If anything, I'd like Lee to slide his cock between my lips again while he pulls on my hair.

"Birth control." He glances over my back at Porter while brushing his thumb along my cheek. "We're claiming you completely, which means we're going to come inside of you."

Birth control? Do my men think I haven't thought this through and know exactly what I want?

Do they not understand I've chosen them, publicly

and privately, and I want to give them everything I have —one hundred percent?

I knew if they accepted me today; it was all or nothing. That's who they are, so that's who I have to be, too.

"I'm covered." I look each man, my men, in the eye. "I want you to come in and on me. You should mark me, claim me, and make me yours forever. You already have my heart. Now, take the rest of me."

Porter and Case grin, but Lee stares at me with something akin to reverence on his face as he continues to stroke my cheek with his thumb. "We have your heart?"

"Are you dense?" I flash him a taunting smile. "I wouldn't waste pink glitter on just anyone. That was from the heart. I love you."

He narrows his eyes and leans forward, kissing me roughly. "I love you, too, pet. And you are going to pay for that later."

I giggle. "Oh, I'm so scared."

Case chuckles, using his thumb and forefinger to bring my face down to his. "You are really asking for it, but I love it. I love you, sweetheart." He kisses me sweetly.

Glancing over my shoulder, I make eye contact with Porter and smile. "Are you going to kiss me and tell me you love me, too?"

He shakes his head. "I do love you, but instead of kissing you, I'm going to make you come."

As if on cue, he pulls the dildo and twists while pushing it back in. I moan, arching my back again and rolling my hips.

"Are you ready to be thoroughly fucked and claimed, Epiphany?" Case asks, as he flexes his fingers into my hips.

"Yes."

Porter drips more lube on my ass and pulls the dildo out at the same time. Then his thumb is there again, massaging in a circular motion. He speeds up as Case pumps his hips faster, fucking me from underneath.

"Lift a little," Case says, sliding his fingers over my clit, sending me rocketing towards my next orgasm.

"Oh," I pant and look up at Lee, opening my mouth and sticking out my tongue to offer him what I hope he wants.

Lee smiles, tightens his grip on my hair and then glides his cock between my lips. "Come for us, pet."

I do, my entire body shaking as Case groans. "Ah, fuck. She's gripping my cock so tight."

Pressure builds at my back entrance, and I know without looking that Porter is there, the blunt head of his cock poised to breach me. He's kneading my ass cheeks, pulling them apart with a gentle massage. "Are you ready, Epi?"

Lee pulls free from my lips, indicating he wants a verbal answer.

I press them together, fear warring with excitement. "Yes."

"Did you like being fucked by the dildo? Did it feel good?" Lee asks.

"Ummm." I hesitate because I'm not sure. It felt good, strange, and overwhelming—all at the same time. I couldn't tell if I wanted to come, go slower, go faster—what? All I know is I wanted something because I was so stimulated and wasn't sure what was going to make me come first. Only when Porter removed the dildo was my mind able to focus on one pleasure over many.

Everyone stops moving.

Case is partially inside me as he holds my hips up and away from him. Lee hooks his finger under my chin, so my eyes come up to meet his. Porter—well, I don't know what he's doing other than standing still, not pushing forward, but not retreating either.

Lee shakes his head. "You didn't like it?"

"I... I did. I can't explain it. It feels good, but strange."

"Maybe we shouldn't do this?" Porter exhales a strangled breath.

"No! I want you to. I want to." I push my hips back and arch my back even more. "Please."

"Why, pet?" Lee asks.

I lick my lips. "Because I want everything with you. There's only one of me and three of you, so I have to do everything I can to satisfy you."

Case chuckles underneath me. "We are satisfied."

"More than satisfied," Porter says. "But if you're scared—"

"I'm not scared." I huff. "I'm overwhelmed and out of my head, like you said I would be."

He raises an eyebrow. "I also said you'd be begging for it."

I huff and roll my eyes. "I said please."

Case smacks my hip. "We need to work on your begging skills."

Jutting my bottom lip, I look through my lashes at Lee and wiggle my ass while pushing back against Porter. "Pleeeaaaassseeeee."

Porter runs his thumb with more lube across my asshole.

Case taps his finger against my clit. He pulls out of me and reaches up to cup the back of my head, bringing my lips crushing down on his. He kisses me breathlessly, distracting me, consuming me, devouring me—and I love it.

"I want you to push back on me, baby, as I push forward." Porter says, the head of his cock once again pushing against my most delicate opening.

"What?" I murmur against Case's lips.

"Just enough to do the opposite of clenching, which you are doing right now."

I try to focus on relaxing, opening for Porter, who pushes forward to breach the tight ring of muscle. Gasping, I rest my forehead against Case's lips.

He kisses me. "Good girl."

"Ah, fuck baby. Don't clench." Porter moves the tiniest bit in and out. He's so gentle, all I feel is full. So delectably full, it doesn't take long for my gasps to turn into moans.

Case chuckles. "I think our little brat likes it."

"She's got me in a vice grip," Porter curses, pushing in further with each stroke.

"How do you feel, pet?" Lee strokes my head.

I look up at him sitting above our heads with his knees splayed and his cock utterly ignored. "I want more."

He flashes me a dazzling smile. "We're about to give you more. A lot more."

Case is sliding the head of his cock back and forth across my swollen pussy lips when Porter says, "How does that feel, baby?"

"More." I push back, realizing his hips are against my ass.

He slides out and then back in, over and over, until I feel nothing but pleasure coursing through my limbs. "She's ready, Case."

Case pushes in at the same time that Porter pulls out. Then they alternate, one pushing as the other pulls, keeping me full and satiated. It feels so good that a guttural groan rips free from my throat as my clit rubs against Case's fingers.

Lee hooks his finger under my chin and lifts my head. "Are you ready for me, pet?"

"Yes." I nod, my eyes half open as the overwhelming pleasure makes me lightheaded. Parting my lips, I flatten my tongue and offer him my mouth. He slides in, gathering my hair in a loose ponytail and pulling tight as my three men fill me in every way possible. Not just my body, which is certainly being used, but also my heart as it swells with the love and care they show me.

I've seen my fair share of debauchery. Walked in on orgies, attended fetish balls, been to live sex shows in Amsterdam, but I never thought the women being devoured by multiple men were treasured or adored. Now that I'm the woman being consumed, I understand the love and care the men had for their lady. There is no way this much pleasure could come from men who didn't care. I feel their love with every stroke, every kiss, every nibble—even every smack.

The pressure within me builds as another orgasm crests, but this one feels different. I'm not sure where it's coming from or how I'm going to let it go. It builds until I'm on the verge of tears, desperate to come but unable to release.

"Jesus, she's got me locked in tight." Case says at the same time he and Porter quicken their strokes, chasing their own releases.

"Are you going to come for us, pet? Are you going to come for your men?" Lee asks while he too thrusts faster, deeper into my mouth, causing tears to spill down my cheeks.

Through blurry vision, I moan and cast him a pair of pitiful eyes. I want to come so badly, but I don't think I know how.

"Fuck!" Porter barks, shooting his load deep inside of me. He fills me, his fingers digging into my hips while Case continues to thrust his hips up into me. It's once Porter is unmoving that my orgasm takes over, my entire body convulsing while filled by all three of my men.

Case groans and shoots his load deep into my pussy, fucking me through it with hard, deep strokes. The three of us are trembling, or maybe I'm shaking them with my full body convulsion, when I remember Lee needs an extra bit of attention. I hollow my cheeks and suck him hard, laying my breasts against Case's chest so I can wrap my fingers around his cock and bring him to completion.

He tightens his grip on my hair and pulls tight, a nice bite of pain letting me know he is close, too.

"Good girl," he groans as he shoots his seed down my throat. I gobble every drop before he slips free from my mouth and leans down while pulling my head back, claiming my lips. "A very good girl."

I smile, collapsing onto Case's chest when Lee lets my hair go. Porter pulls out of me and then wipes me clean with a cool wet cloth before crawling onto the bed to lie beside us. He brushes the hair out of my face while I press my cheek against Case's pec.

I turn and stare into Porter's mesmerizing gray eyes. "You did so good, baby."

Case falls out of me, his cum dripping out of my pussy. He wraps his arms around me, squeezing me with a sweet hug, and whispers into my ear. "Fucking love you, sweetheart."

I've spent ten years hiding in plain sight. I've been the party girl, a model, an entrepreneur, and an influencer. Even with five million followers who claim to love me, none of them know the real me. But tonight, with these three men, I feel seen and loved.

I will never give up this feeling.

I will never give them up.

Finally, I have my family.

Finally, I feel like I'm home.

ENTES TUERE
PUNIRE IMPIOS

EPIPHANY

"How did it go?" Lee stands as we come off the elevator. He pulls me into his arms and kisses the top of my head.

"I'm going to take that photographer's nuts the next time I see him," Case grumbles, predictably dropping both of our bags on the floor.

I sigh. "You can't threaten the photographers. None of them are going to work with me if you keep snarling at them."

"He had no fucking reason to touch you like he did," Case growls and then shakes his head, turning his attention to Lee. "You should have seen this asshole. He kept adjusting her top, grabbing her hips to move her this way or that. Openly flirting with her as if the rest of us weren't there."

Case points his finger at me. "He didn't touch any of the other models nearly as much as he handled you."

Rolling my eyes, I push out of Lee's arms and wave my hands, dismissing both of them. "Whatever you say."

"Someone's feeling feisty." Lee raises his brow.

"Someone needs their ass beat," Case retorts.

"I'm so scared." I wiggle my fingers and dance around the sofa, putting the piece of furniture between us.

Case isn't wrong. Phillip adjusted my clothes, my hair, and my stance—a lot. He manhandled me as much as possible, given the circumstances, but what Case doesn't know is that Phillip did it because I asked him to.

I haven't needled my men in months. Between my work and their work, we've been pulled in a dozen different directions and rarely have time to be *together* together. They've made sure I'm never alone, escorting me across the globe on different shoots, and accompanying me to business meetings in New York and Los Angeles. I rarely spend a night alone, and when I do, it's because I'm staying at my father's estate with Leti—a bit of family time while my men work out-of-town details.

However, my days of attending red carpet events or celebrity parties to fill my time and my heart are over. I'll take a night snuggled up on the couch with one or all of my men over champagne and yachts any day.

Porter comes out of our upstairs bedroom and stares down at us from the second floor, which is really the fifth floor. "What's going on?"

"Our brat is begging to be punished." Case pulls off his shirt.

"Is she?" Porter grins and winks at me. "I love it when she does that."

"You have to catch me first," I taunt.

Lee spreads his arms. "Where are you going to go, pet?"

I crouch down and reach under the couch for the tray of silly string I put there before we left two days ago, but it's missing.

Porter chuckles and waves a can. "Looking for something?"

"You found my stash?"

"Baby, who do you think you're dealing with?"

I stick out my bottom lip. "You guys are no fun."

"We could be, if you'd stop running." Lee stalks me from the left, which is exactly what I hoped he would do, considering I plan to distract Case with his luggage and then make a dash down the stairs to my right.

"Have you checked your bag, Case?"

He narrows his eyes. "What about my bag?"

I shrug and plaster on my sweetest smile—the one that doesn't fool my men in the least. Lee stops stalking me and watches as Case bends down and pulls the zipper back, a puff of pink chalk dust blowing up in his face.

"What the fuck did you do?"

I laugh as I make a dash for the stairwell. "It's non-toxic and machine washable!"

Instead of running downstairs, as they expect me to do, I take the stairs up to the sixth floor, which is empty. A giant open space with nothing except windows and concrete.

Only when I burst through the door, it's not empty. It's fully equipped as a sound studio with a makeup counter and storage for all my boxes, as well as a dressing area with a photography stage, complete with lighting and backdrops.

Porter comes out of the stairwell behind me, wrapping his arms around my waist and nuzzling his mouth against my neck. "Surprise, baby."

"What is all this?" I whisper as the elevator doors open and Lee and Case, with pink chalk all over his face, exit the car.

"You've been talking about needing a studio. We had the space here, so we tried to create for you what we saw in your apartment on your father's estate."

Lee and Case walk across the expansive open floor plan toward us. "We know you'll want to put your feminine touches on everything, but since you ruined the surprise and ran up here, I guess you've opened your Christmas present early."

My mouth is agape as I take everything in. There is so much space up here, I can easily break this up into many sound stages for different purposes. "I thought you wanted me to limit my time online, not increase it."

"Sure, it stresses us out when you put yourself out there. Your fame and beauty are only going to attract more whackos as time goes by and you become more famous. However, we would never stop you from pursuing your dreams or accomplishing your goals," Lee says.

"And so, if we can help you do that from the security of our home, even better," Case adds.

I smile, staring at the pink chalk speckled across his

face. "I have been thinking about doing a series about men and makeup."

Case narrows his eyes. "Don't even fucking think about it."

Laughing, I wiggle my ass against Porter's semi-erect cock. "And maybe a line of gray sweatpants."

"Are you trying to make us jealous?" he asks.

"I think she's trying to goad us into spanking her," Lee adds.

Porter slides his hand down my belly and inside my pants, his finger deftly gliding through my arousal to find my clit. "I think she needs to be fucked, but instead of asking for it, she's provoking us."

Lee steps forward and fists a handful of my hair, pulling my head back so I have no choice but to look at him while Porter teases my clit with slow and lazy circles of his finger. "Maybe we should deny you. It's been a while since we have denied you an orgasm, pet."

I shake my head, my eyes wide. "I was kidding. No gray sweatpants. No men's makeup lines."

"Hmmm." Lee swings me up into his arms and turns us toward Case. "Well, brother, you've endured her shenanigans over the last couple of days... what punishment does she deserve?"

Case runs his hand over his hair, shaking loose some of the chalk. "I'd like her to wash this pink shit off of me before sinking to her knees in the shower to suck my cock."

"That seems fair."

"Or..." Porter says over his shoulder as he walks to a door hidden in a wall behind the backdrops and green screens. "Case could suck it up, and we could introduce Epi to what's behind door number one."

"I like that idea even better," Lee growls, his chest reverberating with his pleasure.

Case grins, and it's the evil grin—the one that promises punishment before pleasure. "I can deal."

As soon as Lee walks toward the door, I squirm in his arms, positive I'm going to love what's coming.

But I can't let them know that.

That would defeat the purpose.

Plus, they love it when I fight.

Lee switches his hold on me effortlessly, swinging me over his shoulder and carrying me caveman style with his forearm wrapped over my knee, my head hanging over his back.

Case takes the opportunity as he brings up the rear to fist a handful of my hair and pull my head back, meeting me in the eye. "I will see you on your knees in the shower before we go to bed tonight."

I lick my lips. "Yum."

He shakes his head and kisses me hard.

We enter a room that is dimly lit in comparison with the rest of the floor; the windows covered in a privacy film.

Lee sets me down as the door clicks shut behind us. I look around and realize they partitioned off the entire southwest wall of the building with drywall, turning nine hundred of the thirty-six hundred square feet into a play-room worthy of The Access Club.

"Oh, my." I can't think of anything more appropriate to say.

In the middle of the room is a St. Andrews Cross with padded supports. Next to it is a black leather bondage horse. Hanging on the wall are a variety of paddles, flog-gers, blindfolds, and ropes. Porter has become interested in Shibari as of late, so I'm guessing those are his. Between that and the wall is a king-sized bed, perfect for this room, but not nearly large enough for us to sleep together, and a dresser with maybe half of our sex toys displayed on top.

"When did you do this?" I breathe, running my fingers over the paddles, some of which are new.

"We did the construction while you were in Puerto Rico with Porter two months ago. And we've been working on it here and there ever since." Lee smacks my ass and then grabs his favorite paddle off the wall, a wicked gleam in his eye.

My three men slowly crowd around me, Porter now also shirtless, with his joggers hanging low on his hips.

"There's something I should tell you before we get started." I bite my lip and look down, pretending I'm remorseful when I'm anything but. I know what I did was risky, but I'm betting the reward will be worth it.

"Yes, pet?"

"Phillip and I—" I twist my hands together "—before the photoshoot, when we were in the dressing room where Case couldn't see us..."

The smile on Case's face drops and his eyes narrow. "I asked my gay photographer, who has been in a loving relationship for over four years, to fuss over me as much as possible so I could ensure my man pinned me against the wall and fucked me senseless when we got home."

"You asked him to paw at you?" Case says through gritted teeth.

"That's a very dangerous game to play with men like us, pet." Lee's cheeks flush red, the vein in his forehead bulging.

"There are better ways to get our attention, baby." Porter shakes his head in disappointment.

"But I got your attention," I point out.

"You almost got Phillip's balls cut off. Gay or straight, he wouldn't be much use to anyone if I got to do any of the things simmering in my head for the last three hours."

Lee shakes his head and spins me to face the cross, my back end exposed to them. He and Porter make quick work of my wrists, securing them high over my head. They pull my pants down my legs and over my tennis shoes, leaving me shackled, bare-assed in a tank top and vintage Converse high tops. They put a spreader bar between my ankles, and then Lee slides a blindfold over my eyes.

I protest, and his hand slides over my mouth. "Do you want to be gagged too?"

There is very little I mind my men doing to me, but I don't enjoy being gagged. "No."

"Then shut up."

I press my lips together, thinking maybe I pushed my

men a little too far this time. Case hasn't said a word, nor has he touched me, and I usually get kisses while I'm being strung up. No kisses, not even from Porter, who is definitely the gentlest of the three.

Rough hands pull my ass back, and I brace for the sharp sting of a paddle, but instead, they wrap straps around my waist and between my legs, securing the small butterfly clit vibrator we bought a couple of weeks ago. It's remote controlled, and I know I set them to truly torture me for my transgressions.

And then... there is nothing.

No one is touching me.

No one is talking.

No one moves about the room.

I'm lost in a vacuum of nothingness without my eyesight.

"Where are you?" I finally blurt out. I can't help myself.

The vibrator kicks on for five seconds before turning off, just enough to tease, but not enough to build toward an orgasm.

I hiss, jerking my hips. "Talk to me."

More silence followed by a longer vibration. This one is maybe ten seconds. Just long enough to cause me to try to squeeze against the vibrator and add more pressure, more friction, but with the spreader bar keeping my ankles more than shoulder width apart, and my arms tethered above to stop me from bending forward, that proves impossible.

"Dammit." I hiss, true frustration building within me.

They yank my hair hard, and Case is growling in my ear. "You will stand here and take this torture as payment for tormenting me like you did. You will not come; we will make sure of it. Then you will take a spanking as your punishment for being a brat in general. And maybe, if you take both very well, maybe we'll let you come. But not until after we've come first."

"Take this time to think about how you push our buttons and what behavior we reward versus punish," Lee says from some distance away.

"I'm going to take a shower. Then, maybe we'll get something to eat. We might even watch a show or something while you stand here and think about what you did. No amount of bitching, moaning, or whining will save you this time." Case smacks me on the ass, and then I hear the door close.

Did they actually leave me alone? Really?

They set the vibrator to low, kicking on for ten seconds every twenty seconds, just long enough to build pressure, but not nearly long or strong enough to make me come. I'm going out of my mind within minutes, cursing them with increased vigor.

"Okay. I'm sorry."

Nothing.

"Guys? This is not okay."

More nothing.

"Are you fucking kidding me? Did you really leave me here alone?"

Absolute silence.

I cry, actual tears building in my eyes as the vibrator

kicks up to high. "I promise to never use jealousy to get your attention again!"

Finally, hot breath blows across my wet thighs.

"She's fucking soaked," Porter says, and I can't help but arch my back toward him.

Lee smacks my ass cheek hard, backing me down. I know his big hand, rough and calloused from years of hard work. "You better not have come."

"Please," I whine.

"What exactly are you begging for, pet?" Lee's voice is close, but still, no one touches me.

"I'm sorry."

"Yeah, I bet you are. If I were strung up like you, brought to and kept on the edge of release for twenty minutes, I'd be sorry, too."

Twenty minutes? It feels like a lifetime.

Case's fresh spring-scented shampoo fills the surrounding air, letting me know that he definitely left long enough to take a shower. "Do you have something to say to me, sweetheart?"

"I'm sorry," I whimper.

He sighs, nuzzling my neck with his soft lips. "Are you ready for your spanking?"

"Please." I'm desperate to receive my punishment so we can move on to making up when I can wrap my arms around him, pull him close, and pepper his face with kisses.

The restraints on my wrists move down, allowing my arms to drop to chest level. I flex my hands, my fingers tingling as blood rushes into them. They pull my hips back and slide a padded bench in front of me, my thighs pressed against the cool leather and firm foam.

With the pad at the right angle, I can press the vibrator against my clit, giving me the little extra oomph I desperately need to release. But my men are smarter than that, and with one gentle roll of my hips, the vibrator falls to the floor between my feet.

"Oh, hell no," Case says.

I can see nothing, which only amplifies everything else.

Every sound.

Every breath taken near me, its origin left a secret.

They pull my tank top up so my belly is flush with the leather. My breasts are adjusted so they lie on top of the pad. Firm fingers pinch and roll my nipples, and I don't need my eyesight to know it's Porter. He'll mark me tonight, knowing I don't have another photoshoot scheduled until April.

"Ready?" Lee says before tapping my ass with his paddle.

"I can't see," I object.

"We know," Case says before delivering his own smack to my ass, his much harder than Lee's.

Porter latches on to my nipple, biting and teasing me with his teeth.

"Ahhh!" I cry out as Lee delivers another smack, followed quickly by Case.

"Let's hear it, pet," Lee says, delivering a third swat with no soothing rubs, no gentle caress of my burning flesh.

"Hear what?" I snap, truly frustrated this time. I think they are taking this punishment a little far—making it last way longer than necessary.

Lee smoothes my hair back and runs his nose up my throat, chuckling darkly in my ear. "You know what I want to hear."

Case lands a blow, causing me to yelp.

"Please."

"Please what?" Porter says, his breath on my chest.

"Please fuck me."

"And?" Case growls.

"Please mark me, claim me, and remind me who I belong to."

"Who do you belong to, pet?"

"You. Only you," I cry out.

"We're going to take you hard and fast, chasing our release, solely focusing on our pleasure. There is nothing gentle about what we are going to do to you tonight. Do you understand?"

"Yes."

"You deserve this, you know?" Case says.

"I know." Most women would be terrified by the words coming out of their mouths, but not me. I want their hands on me, any way I can get them, and they truly don't scare me because I know they love me with all their hearts.

These men would kill for me.

They would die for me.

And while they will take out their frustrations with

me on my body, they will reward me in the end, despite their vows to the contrary.

Case slides his fingers along my exposed pussy, growling before plunging two fingers deep inside of me. "Fuck me. I can't help myself."

I moan, fighting to hide the smile threatening to spread my lips.

Porter leans forward and whispers in my ear, a teasing lilt to his tone, like he's trying not to smile or laugh. "Don't you dare like it, baby."

Biting my lip, I shake my head and moan no—as if I'm fooling anyone.

They release my wrists from the cross and pull them behind my back; the cuffs tethered together. Then they remove the spreader bar pushing my ankles apart, and I'm lifted and carried to the bed, only to be tossed unceremoniously onto the plush mattress.

"Heads or tails?" Porter says.

With my hands tied behind my back and a blindfold in place, I lie there like a sack of potatoes, awaiting my fate.

"Heads," Case says as the mattress dips above my head.

Lee's strong fingers grip my thigh and swing me up to straddle his waist. I'm instantly impaled on his cock, his forceful thrust ripping a cry from my throat.

Case fists a handful of my hair, pulling my head back. "Open."

His tone brokers no argument, my lips parting on his

command. He slides his beautiful dick in, fucking my mouth without preamble.

Slick, cool lube drips over my ass, and then Porter shoves his lubricated fingers in, pumping a few times before lining up the head of his cock and moving with more care than either Case or Lee has handled me. But it doesn't take but a few seconds for him to fully seat himself inside of me, my insides quivering with pent-up release on the fringe of spilling over.

Lee stops moving, his fingers digging into my hips. "Don't you dare come."

I'd love to answer him, but Case is busy fucking my mouth, hitting the back of my throat without care as tears spill down my cheeks.

"Epi! Don't you fucking dare come," Lee growls.

I shake my head.

There is no use in yelling at me about it. If he and Porter pump in and out of me a couple more times, I'm going to come.

I can't stop it.

I won't stop it.

"Ahhh," Lee hisses as I clench down on him. "Fuck it."

He and Porter fuck me with reckless abandon, striving to beat me to the finish line and reach their own orgasm before I do. The dam within me breaks loose the moment Case shoots a load of cum down my throat. My pussy clamps down on Lee, causing him to join me in my release while Porter continues to pump his hips forward, leaning over and biting my back as he comes.

An almost photo-finish tie.

They can't be mad at me for that, can they?

Case lets go of my hair, and I collapse on Lee's chest, my hands still tied behind me. Porter relaxes behind me, his hot breath skimming over the sweat beading up on my lower back. They pull the blindfold from my eyes, my mascara smeared down my cheeks, my eyelashes clumped together. I blink repeatedly, trying to clear my vision and take in my men's faces.

Case rubs his finger over my cheek and shakes his head at me. "You're lucky we love you as hard as we do; otherwise, we'd have to punish your inability to follow directions."

Porter undoes my cuffs, letting my arms fall free. Lee rolls me to his side between them. "You just can't help yourself, can you, pet?"

"What did you expect? You tease and edge me for a half-hour and then fill me with your glorious cocks, pounding into me mercilessly. How was I not going to orgasm?"

Lee strokes his fingers down my cheek. "I guess we will have to work on your training."

"No," I say definitively.

He arches his brow. "No?"

"No," I say again, shaking my head to look over my shoulder at Porter, who has stopped nibbling on my neck. "Training how not to orgasm doesn't sound like fun at all."

Case sighs and stretches out above us, one hand propping up his head, the other playing with locks of my hair. "She's got a point."

"Whose side are you on?" Lee grumbles.

"I didn't say she was right. Only that she has a point."

We fall into a comfortable silence, my boneless body comfortably sandwiched between two of my men, while my third plays with my hair. "I love each of you more than I thought I could love another."

"We love you, too." Lee smiles and places a chaste kiss against my lips.

"I have a question for you." I sit up so I can meet all three of their eyes easily.

"What's that, baby?" Porter reaches out and strokes my thigh.

Biting my lip, I take a deep breath and steel my nerves. "I want to get married, but I don't know how we would do that."

My men sit up with me. Lee's brow furrows. "You want to get married?"

Nodding, I look each of them in the eye, making sure they understand how serious I am. "I hate introducing you as my boyfriend, or as my bodyguard, or, god forbid, when we are all together, my security team. I hate not going out as a group except to The Access Club. I don't care what other people think. I'm happy. I'm in love. My sister and my father know what's up, and even if Walter hates it, the rest of the world can bite my ass if they have a problem with my lifestyle choices."

"Biting your ass is my job, baby." Porter throws me a wink.

"You'd rather introduce us as your husbands?" Case asks.

"Yes."

Lee moves to the edge of the bed and pulls me into his lap. Porter and Case sit on either side of him, touching me. "If you want to get married, we'll marry you tomorrow, pet. Legally, you'd marry one of us, but under the eyes of the gods, you are already ours, and we belong to you."

"A piece of paper means nothing to us," Case says as he strokes my hair. "It will not change our devotion to you. The people who know you call you our wife. If you want to introduce us as your husband, you are free to do so."

"Unless this is about having an actual wedding complete with flowers and cake?" Porter arches his brow.

"And vows," I throw in a little too quickly.

Lee smiles and nods his head, pressing a kiss on my neck. "And vows."

"Are we talking about a public or private affair?"

"Private." I bite my lip, the truth coming out piece by piece. And then I can't stop the words from spilling out of me in rapid succession. "The four of us and maybe another four who get married on the same beach, at the same time, while vacationing on the same tropical island together."

Case laughs, falling back and resting a hand on his belly. "I think we're being played, gentlemen. Do Reese, Caiden, or Soren know what you and your sister have been up to?"

"If they don't yet, they will soon."

Porter shakes his head, a big smile spreading his lips, his gray eyes sparkling with amusement. "A double wedding. Two brides and six grooms. I bet that's never happened before in the history of ever never."

Lee shrugs. "If that's what you want, pet, that's what you'll get. Have you already planned this little soirée?"

"No. Not yet. We started talking about it last week while you were out of town. Leti doesn't even know I'm bringing it up today, and I don't know when she's going to talk to them about it, so don't say anything."

"Oh, hell no," Lee chuckles. "I'm not going to be the one to break this to them."

"Although it would be fun to see their faces when it comes up." Case laughs again.

I glance between them. "Do you think they will tell her no?"

Porter rubs my thigh and shakes his head. "They can't tell her no anymore than we can tell you no. If you want a double wedding on the beach overlooking the ocean, then that's what you'll get."

"But we are not sharing a house with them for the honeymoon," Lee says sharply. "I don't care how close you and your sister have become; you do not want her hearing the things we do to you on our wedding night."

I squeeze his neck. "Thank you, my husbands. I love you."

Saying the words, hearing them roll off my tongue, I realize I've been waiting for this milestone to solidify our family unit. I've never doubted their feelings for me, or my feelings for them, but maybe after a lifetime of casual relationships and meaningless flings globe-trotting around the world, deep down I worried that this too would prove temporary.

But my men, whether my antics annoy or amuse them, are dedicated to standing by me.

Publicly, privately, they are mine and I am theirs—forever.

ENTES TUERE
PUNIRE IMPIOS

Second Epilogue

LEE

Standing barefoot on a sandy beach next to Case and Porter wasn't outside the realm of possibilities, but I never thought I'd be standing across from Reese, Caiden, and Soren while we wait for *our* brides to walk down the aisle.

On paper, Epiphany and I are married in the state of Illinois, but this ceremony is what truly matters—where the rubber hits the road, or the wind moves the tide, as the case may be.

Porter snorts and shakes his head at Caiden, who is making faces at us.

Reese smacks Caiden in the arm and then looks at me, shrugging with a look of *what are you going to do?*

I can't believe our women wanted an actual ceremony, and a double one, at that.

But here we are.

Six of us standing up waiting for our brides to walk down the aisle.

And not just an aisle carved in the sand for the ceremony's sake, but an actual pathway cut between people here to wish the happy new families a joyous union.

If you think finding a preacher who would bless this holy unity would be impossible to find, you'd be right. Luckily, we know a guy who got ordained online as a joke for his brother's wedding five years ago. Royal is ex-PsySpecOps, works for Victor in the Southwest region, and is here with his two partners, Jayson and Baehr.

I think they wanted to come to see what a spectacle like this looks like. Normally I wouldn't have been down with inviting anyone, but what Epi wants, Epi gets. Plus, Royal being ordained worked out in our favor and guaranteed him an invitation.

After allowing that to happen, I lost any semblance of control.

In the small crowd is Epi and Leti's father, Walter, as well as a few select members of Epi's entourage—aka, close friends—as well as our boss Victor, Victor's business partner Jacob (another ex-PsySpecOps unit member) who runs the Arizona office, with his lady Patty-Ann.

And because Epiphany really wanted this to be a party, we invited the guys down south who only work with us when we have more work than we can handle. Ken, LaRoux, and Paddy from Mountain Love, Tennessee, and Stiles, Bastion, and Romeo from Nashville.

They only arrived this afternoon, so we haven't had a chance to catch up. It's been years since we served together, but Ken and his crew showed up with a sassy little blonde between them, while Stiles has a protective arm around an innocent-looking brunette. Without knowing their stories, I can guarantee you their situations are similar to ours.

Even the guys from New York showed up with a cute redhead between them. Darian, Xander, and Garrett turned down Victor when they separated, choosing to start their own security firm in the heart of Manhattan. I have no idea where they got the funds for that venture. Technically, they are a direct competitor of Townsend Security Agency—but they don't want to grow beyond the caseload the three of them can handle.

Regardless, I'm pretty sure Victor is still pissed they told him no.

Men like us don't handle hearing no nearly as well as we should.

I glance around at the assembled mass, itchy to get this shindig underway. Twenty men plus others, all of whom know what's up.

This is crazy. Eight PsySpecOps units in one place. For our wedding! As Porter once said—two brides and six grooms has never happened before in the history of ever never.

"Are you going to make it?" Case glances at me.

"Yeah. You?"

"I'm not nervous about getting married. I'm more worried about what kind of shit Epi's going to pull at the last minute. You know she's going to do something that warrants a spanking in front of all these people."

"Yeah, I know."

"I found a case of silly string in our suite," Porter says casually.

Too casually.

"You didn't think that was pertinent information to share with the rest of us?" I snap.

He shrugs. "I took care of it."

"That's probably why they are late. She's probably tearing up the island looking for that silly string." Case chuckles.

They're probably late because it was the most subdued way Epi can antagonize us without embarrassing her sister.

"Spank her ass later?" Case says with a gleam in his eye.

"Definitely."

Prince's "Sexy Muthafucker" comes on in the distance, but considering no one else is on this private beach besides us, I know it's Epi.

I flush red and lower my eyes to the ground, shaking my head.

Porter laughs, joined by Caiden who points at us and says, "That's definitely for you."

Yeah, no shit.

No traditional wedding march for our brides because that would be boring, and Epi is not about being boring. Honestly, I'm kind of surprised I haven't seen a helicopter with photographers circling the beachfront. She's joked about going public with our relationship, but I keep reminding her she doesn't want to deal with the long-term ramifications of outing us. We might not give a fuck what other people think—if people close to us figure it out, they figure it out—but corporate sponsors, consumers, and her five plus million followers are not nearly as woke as she thinks they are.

And I don't even want to think about what kind of hassle it would present us when we do our jobs.

Epi and Leti walk out of the bridal suite holding hands and wearing similar white lace sundresses, but as is Epi's style, hers is considerably shorter and hugs every curve.

Even though I'm used to her prancing around in near nothing at the house, she still takes my fucking breath away.

"Holy hell." Case exhales.

The full weight of what we're doing hits me at this moment.

I never thought I'd get married.

Never thought I'd stand up in front of friends or family.

Never thought I'd look down an aisle as my bride walked towards me.

Once I met Case and Porter, I figured my life would play out differently. They instantly became my family, but deep down I feared we'd never find a woman who'd accept us, much less claim us publicly. Even though we've been together for eighteen months, it isn't until this moment I realized somewhere in the back of my mind, I've been waiting for it to fall apart.

"She's really ours," Porter murmurs.

I guess I'm not the only one having an out-of-body experience.

Epi locks eyes with us—her smile only for us—a light blush to her cheeks. She steps up to me, but Case and Porter flank her, each kissing her cheek and neck.

"You are stunning," Case says.

"Pure perfection," Porter agrees.

"An absolute angel," I add.

She giggles and raises her brow. "We all know that's not true."

Smiling, I nod. "I'll amend. You look like an angel."

Case chuckles darkly. "Even the devil presents as the most beautiful of all angels."

"That sounds like me." She rises on her toes and kisses me on the lips.

Royal leans forward and says, "I didn't get to that part yet."

I divert my eyes over her head and narrow them at him. "Then hurry up."

He leans back with a big cheesy grin, claps his hands, and says in a booming voice. "Let's get this boat in the water."

CASE

Lee and Epiphany were married in a civil union two weeks ago at the Cook County courthouse. Porter and I were there to sign on the dotted lines as witnesses, not husbands, for obvious reasons. It would be a lie to say I haven't harbored a smidge of jealousy, a touch of green rage coursing through my veins, since that day.

I mean, I understand. Legally, she can only be married to one of us. Lee was the obvious choice. He's an only child and both of his parents died years ago.

My family, after an unfortunate confrontation at my parent's fortieth anniversary celebration with my sister, knows the basics—Lee, Porter, and I are in a relationship with Epiphany. That's about as much detail as I could give my mother while looking her in the eye, or more to the point, while she could look me in the eye.

I told them I love Epiphany with all my heart, and I also love Lee and Porter.

They are my family.

My brothers.

My best friends—and sharing the woman we love works for us.

Unfortunately, they haven't wrapped their brains around our family dynamics and I haven't felt the need to make them understand.

Six months ago I got an invitation in the mail for my parent's celebration. I knew it was coming, but hadn't told the others about it because I wasn't sure how we should approach it. If we didn't have Epiphany in our lives, I would have attended with my two best friends, like we have multiple times over our fifteen year friendship, but Epi presented a new variable to our dynamic.

Let's face it, she's not known for behaving herself in the public eye.

For the longest time, my sister thought I was gay, and that Lee and Porter were my lovers. Why she thought that, I don't know, because she never asked me about my love life directly. While she accepted that scenario—me and my two gay lovers living together for fifteen years—our actual relationship with Epi dumbfounds her.

When we brought Epi to my parent's fortieth wedding anniversary in Colorado—because once she saw the invitation she begged me to take her—we introduced her as my girlfriend and left it at that. But you know she couldn't keep her hands off Lee and Porter, so it wasn't long before my sister was pulling me into my old bedroom to inform me that my girlfriend was cheating on me with my best friends.

I tried to explain our relationship to her and her only response was, "How?"

That is still her response to this day, hence why I didn't invite her to our wedding. Actually, I didn't invite any of them. I'm not mad at their lack of understanding or acceptance. I think this is a lot to take in for most people, but I don't have the energy to convince them this is right for me or prove how happy I am.

Now that Epi is standing in front of me, all the jealousy I've harbored over the last few weeks dissipates. She's about to be mine—ours—but also mine. Sure, one could say she was already mine, but something about having her and Lee put it on paper broke our connection in my mind, even though neither of them said anything to make me doubt our commitment.

She throws me a wink, as if she knows the feelings vibrating within me, making me itch to pull her into my arms and kiss her breathless.

The four of us stand in a circle, Epi's back to Royal as he begins.

"I'm glad the brides started the ceremony with Prince. This allows me to start my part with: Dearly beloved, we are gathered here today to discuss this thing called life..." Royal flashes us a cheesy ass grin. "Just kidding."

I remember him being a prankster, not that we had a lot of interaction back in the day, but I might hurt him if he repeats the entire intro to Let's Go Crazy.

"So... this is different." Royal glances between our two assembled groups, his face taking on a more serious note. "But, love is love. Men like us rarely get blessed with meeting a woman who can put up with one of us, much less all three. You, gentlemen, have beat the odds. Regardless of what god or goddess you pray to, someone is smiling down on you, blessing you, forgiving you for your past sins, and bestowing upon you a prosperous future full of love and happiness. Don't take it for granted. Not one damn day. Cherish your friendship, your bond, your brotherly love, and the love of your woman—the strength of which most people will not experience in their lifetime."

Facing us, Epi is using her left hand to hold my right hand with her other hand in Porter's. Lee stands between us with his hands clasped in front of him, a concession he makes, I suppose, because he got to put his name on the piece of paper. This is awkward—although Royal's words are poignant and will stick with me for a long time—and why relationships like ours don't normally have formal ceremonies.

Epi must sense my nervousness, because she waggles her eyebrows, her facial movements so slight they are imperceptible to everyone else but the three of us who can read the mischief brewing in her brain before she's fully planned out her scheme.

I squeeze her hand and mouth, *behave yourself.*

She juts out her bottom lip, but her eyes sparkle with true happiness.

Royal continues. "I'm thrilled to be here today to witness, not one, but two happy unions. The couples have prepared their own vows, so we'll start with Epiphany and her Neanderthals—"

My head snaps up and eyes go straight to Royal, who is chuckling and holding up a three by five index card. "Her words, man. They are on the cue card."

Lee growls so low, even I can barely hear it. "You are going to get it later."

Epi's smile widens. "I hope so."

At this moment, I'm glad we turned our backs to the crowd, so they can only see a portion of the blush hitting my neck.

I start. "Epiphany, we knew we were in trouble the moment we laid eyes on you. Not only are you beautiful, but you challenged us from the minute we met—and men like us need a strong woman who tests us daily in our lives."

Porter nods. "You are perfect for us, encompassing everything we knew we wanted but never thought we'd find in one woman."

Lee clears his throat. "We vow to be everything you need and mostly what you want."

"We are your biggest fans, completely devoted to you," I say.

"We're talking Swiffy-level devotion." Porter grins, causing Epi to giggle.

"And we're here to support you, protect you, and love you," Lee says.

"Forever," the three of us say together.

"I know you will." Epi presses her lips together, her eyes watery. "I feared I'd never have a true connection with one man, much less three who get me and accept me as I am. Horrible circumstances brought us together, but through it I was gifted a new lease on life filled with love, affection, and friendship. You love me as I am, despite all my attention-seeking antics—because, let's face it—we're here now in front of all these people because of my antics." She smiles. "And because you love me for me, I vow to tease and torment you daily, but always with love and kisses. I promise to keep you young and on your toes, and in constant fear of silly string and pink glitter. Forever."

PORTER

Royal moves on to the other group: Reese, Caiden, and Soren, with their bride to be, Leti, but I'm not listening to what they have to say to one another. Instead, I've zoned out the sounds around us and tuned into the water lapping at the shore just beyond. I know this is important to Epi, but honestly, I just want to crawl into bed and fall asleep with her in my arms. That's when the world is at peace and I feel completely whole. Sure, a piece of paper tying us together means something in a court of law, but it doesn't mean dick to my heart. Our woman grabbed it on that first day and hasn't let go of it since.

Besides, the paper isn't between her and I, anyway.

I wish I could tell my family about her, but they are conservative, devout Catholics, and nothing about their commentary while growing up in their home leads me to believe they will comprehend my lifestyle choices. They never understood why I didn't come home after I separated from the military. When I visit, I do it alone, and it eats at me that I'll never be able to introduce Epi to my family—not without a fistful of carefully crafted lies.

But if I want to be happy, I can't force others to accept my choices, nor can I spend a lot of energy trying to convince them to understand. We saw how that went for Case and his family, and I think they handled it like champs compared to how my family would react.

Eh, fuck it. I love my parents, but I'm one of five kids and have been living my own life for over fifteen years. I established my family in Lee and Case, and now we've officially grown by one. How many more will come? Who knows? But I wouldn't mind a big family someday.

Epi squeezes my hand, bringing me back to the here and now. "You okay?" she whispers.

I nod. "Just fine, baby."

"It's almost over." She flashes me a hopeful smile. She knows we'd endure anything for her, but this is definitely not my idea of a good time. Too many people have their eyes on us right now, and while I'm looking forward to drinking a beer and catching up with the guys we served with, I'd rather whisper my sweet nothings in bed—preferably naked and sweaty.

Royal spreads his hands. "Truly beautiful. I had no idea you guys had such poetry within you."

"Fuck off," Reese and Lee grumble at the same time.

"Now that's the balladry I expect." Royal laughs. "Exchange your rings, if you have them."

Epi drops my hand and pulls a long gold chain out from between her breasts. Hanging on the end are three silicon bands in contrasting colors with unique designs. "I know you won't wear these, but I wanted you to have something from me."

She takes them off the chain and offers a graphite gray one with Celtic knots engraving to Case. "For your Irish roots."

Then she offers one that looks like wood grain to Lee. "Because you are strong and unmoving, like an oak." Then she leans forward and whispers, "and because of your favorite paddle."

Then she turns to me and offers me a pearl, green-gray ring with a mountain terrain etching. "Because you take me on wilderness hikes, just the two of us, and the color reminded me of your eyes."

I pull from my pocket a diamond encrusted puzzle ring. "We have something for you, too. Pull this ring apart and it's a mess—unstable, weak, and ill-formed."

"Just like if you were to pull us apart," Case says.

"Assembled, it is whole and beautiful," Lee says.

"That's us, baby." I smile, sliding the ring onto her finger.

She smiles, looking down at her hand. "I love it."

Royal clears his throat and I nod. "With the vows and rings exchanged, and the sun setting behind us, in front of your friends and family, and under the blessings of the gods, I pronounce you family. Brides, take your husbands."

EPIPHANY

I had thought at the end of the ceremony I would do something obnoxious, like throw myself into one of my men's arms and then lay back, making all three hold me up and present me to the crowd—but now, I want nothing more than to slip away and be held in their arms in private.

They did this for me.

They endured this crazy ceremony for me.

And not just my three men, but Leti and her men, too.

I mean, this was my crazy idea, after all. Leti agreed, but how much coaxing did I have to do to convince her this was a good idea? I don't even know. I've been bending people to my will for so long, I'm not even conscious of it.

I lift on my toes and place a chaste kiss against Case, then Lee, and then Porter's lips.

My men exchange a look, and Case shakes his head, a mischievous grin parting his lips. "I don't think so, brat."

He pulls me into his arms, bends me back over his forearm, and kisses me hard for the whole crowd, who laugh, hoot, and holler like you'd expect. "That's how we do it in this family."

Porter then pulls me out of Case's arms and lays me out the same way. "We also share in this family."

Lee shakes his head and takes my hand, leading me with a gentle touch out of Porter's arms, pulling me against his chest. "But we don't share with everyone, and they've seen more than enough. You are ours, Epiphany."

I melt into his arms. "Yours. Forever."

"I don't suppose we can blow off the party and take you back to our bungalow?" Porter grins.

Shaking my head, I laugh. "That wouldn't be very nice to our guests."

Then I look over his shoulder to realize all the guests have left their chairs and are moving toward the ballroom with the music and the bartenders. Even the guy presiding over our nuptials, Royal, has left us alone in our private moment. Leti and her men moved toward the water's edge, and we are ultimately alone.

Case chuckles. "You think these guys are going to sit around and watch us love on you? We can take as long as we want. As long as there is food and alcohol, our guests will be fine."

I place my palm on Case's cheek and make eye contact with Porter and Lee. "Thank you for doing this. I know it's weird, but I needed this tidbit of normal in our relationship—ya know?"

"Pizza and movies on Thursday nights aren't normal?" Case arches a brow.

"They are, but they are at home."

"Brunch every other Sunday?" Porter points out.

I side-eye him. "You know what I mean."

"You just wanted a party that celebrated you, pet." Lee runs the back of his fingers over my cheek. "And we're okay with giving you that, because you've given us so much more in return."

"What have I given you besides anxiety and occasional heartburn?" I grin, knowing my words are true and also in jest. When we verbally spar, almost always as a prelude to fun times in the bedroom, they mention anxiety and heartburn—but only with complete affection.

"Love," Lee says.

"Family," Case says

"A home." Porter nods.

I bite my lip to keep the tears at bay. For someone who hadn't cried in ten years, I tear up at the drop of a dime around my men. I guess that's the point of finding yourself cocooned in a loving and accepting connection. You can tear down all the walls you've been protecting your heart with most of your life. With my men, I can finally be vulnerable. "Maybe we should go back to the villa for a bit?"

Lee closes his eyes and takes a deep breath, as if he has to tamp down the desires raging through his body. "If we go to the villa, we are not coming back to the party."

He's right. I know he's right. With three men to satisfy, quickies involving all of us is an impossibility.

"Except, if our wife needs release, I think we should take care of her." Case swings me into his arms and walks to the bride's dressing room—which is no more than a private bathroom off the ballroom—before Lee or Porter can say otherwise. I know Case has been feeling something since Lee and I tied the knot.

Jealousy, perhaps?

Insecurity? I can't imagine why, but I suppose that's a possibility, too.

Things have been a little off between us since the courthouse, but I'm hoping everything will realign once we can be alone tonight.

A triumphant grin spreads across my lips and I squeal before nuzzling my face into Case's neck, his scent warm and inviting, kissed by the ocean breeze.

"Do you need to get off, sweetheart?" he whispers to me.

"I need you."

"You have me. Forever."

He kicks open the bathroom door and glances around. "Holy shit. This is like a small suite. Why are women's bathrooms always so fancy?"

I laugh as he sets my ass down on a plush settee in the middle of the room. He's instantly on his knees in front of me as Lee and Porter shut and lock the door behind them.

"Lift up," Case says as he runs his hands up my thighs.

I bring my ass off the chaise and he hisses. "Naughty girl. Do you guys see this?"

Lee growls. "You don't have on underwear, pet."

"I didn't want panty lines."

Porter licks his lips. "Bullshit. You wanted to give us easy access. Didn't you, baby?"

I bat my lashes. "Maybe."

"Spread your legs." Case doesn't wait for me to comply, and spreads my thighs wide for him. He lowers his head and latches on to my clit with no preamble. I toss my head back and moan, threading my fingers through his thick hair, ripe for release. It's been a few days, the longest I've gone without orgasming since meeting my men. I think we purposely held off for tonight without ever discussing it specifically, but I can't wait any longer.

Porter kneels down on the settee and looms over me, claiming my mouth in an all-consuming kiss. "Come for us, baby."

He doesn't have to ask me twice.

I shatter into a million pieces, coming apart in Case's mouth. Growling between my legs, Case continues to lap his tongue against my pussy, drinking up my come.

"Fuck. Just like cotton candy," he says when he finally comes up for air.

I doubt that's true, but I preen just the same and raise my eyebrow. "You must really like cotton candy because you eat me so well."

"That's because you melt on my tongue." He winks and wipes the back of his mouth.

"How do you feel, pet? Did we take off enough of the edge to see to our guests?"

I run my hand over the bulge in Porter's pants. "Yes, but what about you?"

Porter groans and holds my hand over his hard cock, fighting to not thrust his hips into my open palm.

Lee shakes his head. "We can wait until tonight."

"Fuck you." Porter closes his eyes, his hips gyrating in the tiniest of circles. "I hate waiting."

"Put the beast down for a nap, asshole. We have shit to tend to."

Porter grumbles, pulling me to my feet by my hand. "Fucking people."

I kiss him sweetly. "I'm sorry, baby. Tonight, I will make it up to you."

He pushes my dress down and then smacks my ass. "I know you will."

Lee offers me his hand at the same time Case comes from the sink, wiping his face dry. "Come on, pet. Let's go celebrate our lives."

PSYSPECOPS
INNOCENTES TUERE
PUNIRE IMPIOS

PsySpecOps soldiers aren't like other soldiers.
They aren't even like other special ops units.
They're a cross of special ops, Intel, EXO, Cyber, and
psychological warfare, to name a few.

Imagine if Chuck Norris, MacGyver, and B.F. Skinner
all jerked off into a test tube and then impregnated
Wonder Woman.
That's would be them.

PsySpecOps doesn't take volunteers. They recruit the
best of the best out of the special forces units.

They are chosen not only for their physical prowess—
marksmanship, hand-to-hand, endurance, strength,
intelligence, instinct, and ingenuity—but also for their
psych profile that says they'll work best as a team.

They're the Army's answer to a super soldier without chemical injections and gamma rays.

Together, the three men psychologically profiled to be a team are a near perfect soldier—accentuating each other's strengths and eliminating any weaknesses.

Rumor has it, ex-PsySpecOps teams prefer to find and share one woman versus date independently. It is said to be an unexpected side-effect of their training.

They functional perfectly as one in all other aspects of their life, so why wouldn't they want to offer the perfect woman a complete package?

The Men of PsySpecOps work hard, play hard, and love hard... all they need is to meet the special woman who can handle all they have to give.

IS THAT YOU?

Men of PsySpecOps
OUR WALLFLOWER Queen
Kameron Claire
USA TODAY BESTSELLING AUTHOR

Our Wallflower Queen

I'm the good twin, the quiet one, the one who hides in the shadows. I never draw attention to myself, never cause my family concern, and most people forget I exist. My sister is my polar opposite in every way. Loud and in the spotlight, she likes to let people believe she's the bad twin, but I know better.

So when I'm mistaken for her, kidnapped and thrust into the spotlight, my three gorgeous rescuers, now bodyguards, are my only protection from the attention I've avoided my entire life—and suddenly, I want to be the bad twin.

I want THEIR attention.

I want THEIR affirmation.

I want THEIR praise.

We were hired to rescue and protect the twenty-two year old kidnapped daughter of a billionaire, but none of us expected to fall in love.

She's everything we've been looking for and more, but we're on the job with a timid and traumatized client, and the number one rule as a bodyguard is *Don't lust after the Client*. Although left unstated, we're pretty sure rule number two is *Don't f^ck the Client*. But the more time we spend together, holed up in a rancher smack dab in suburbia, the harder it is to ignore our feelings, especially as she becomes more dependent upon us, seeking the comfort and physical touch she never received growing up.

She has to know what she's doing to us. She wants our attention, and she's got it. But it's more than that. Our good girl has been lonely her whole life—a quelled bird trapped in a gilded cage with no one to take care of her. We are the men to change that.

And as soon as the threat on her life is dealt with, that's what we aim to do.

She's ours to protect, our to cherish, ours to adore.

Men of PsySpecOps
OUR
SCRAPPY
Queen
Kameron Claire
USA TODAY BESTSELLING AUTHOR

I've been stalked by a guy for months who doesn't under the words: Not Interested. But once he escalates his threat by putting my coworker in the hospital, I decide to go on the offensive and give the creep a taste of his own medicine. As a self-proclaimed control freak, I refuse to live in fear and wait for him to come after me. When I sabotage his wooded torture shack, I accidentally blow up the house and the three-month long investigation belonging to the team that's been watching him instead. Of course, I don't know they aren't his goons when we meet, so our introduction consists of me running, cursing, kicking, and punching, only to ultimately lose the fight, but not before I give one a black eye.

We've been tracking this scumbag for three months, waiting for him to lead us to the big fish—the head of the DiFallo human trafficking empire. But when a hellcat blows up our plans, literally, we scoop her up for questioning. She fights us like no woman ever has before, which unfortunately for everyone involved, only turns us on. Her curves are inviting, her tongue is wicked sharp, and her right hook is a thing of beauty—which makes us want to keep her mouth busy while we tether her hands high above her head.

But when we realize she's the scumbag's victim and not an arsonist on DiFallo's payroll, our protective instincts roar to life.

She says she's not interested in our help, but her actions say otherwise, and although we recognize her skill, we can't leave her to take care of this on her own. Not when we're already convinced she belongs with us.

With her life on the line, she has to give up control to us to survive. When she does...

She's ours to protect, ours to fight for, ours to love.

KAMERON CLAIRE
USA TODAY BESTSELLING AUTHOR

Our Incognito Queen

She wants her three gorgeous bosses in the dirtiest way. She's forbidden to them, not only because she's their employee, but because she's too pure to be sullied by their darkest desires.

Can one anonymous night sate their needs and fulfill her fantasies?

My bosses are hot, smart, and totally unattainable. But when I glimpse them at The Access Club—New York's hottest underground sex club—and hear a rumor they share their women, I come up with a plan to live out my fantasy, at least for one night.

We have known each other our entire adult life. Bonded since day one of PsySpecOps training, we now own a successful private security business.

We share everything, and we mean, everything. But the one thing we want to share, we can't, because our sweet girl is too pure for the things we want to do to her. We agreed to leave her alone, but when we get a mysterious invitation in the mail, each of us know we're about to get what we want most in this world—her.

One night won't be enough. She's ours to unveil, ours to pleasure, ours to keep.

Want more **Witty** Tongues, **Wicked** Needs, & **Wild** Deeds?

<u>Veteran K9 Team</u>

** Military Romance **

Mine to Cherish

Mine to Crave

Mine to Possess

Mine to Adore

Mine to Covet

Mine to Worship

Mine to Protect

Mine to Treasure

<u>Hot Nights with the Boss</u>

** Forbidden Office / Age-Gap Romances **

Dating the Boss

Flirting with the Boss

Teasing the Boss

Tempting the Boss

<u>Rangers Football</u>

Sports Romance

Play Action Fake

Quarterback Sneak

Personal Foul

Two-Point Conversion

Red Zone

Man to Man Coverage

The Men of PsySpecOps

Reverse Harem Romance

Our Bratty Queen

Our Wallflower Queen

Our Scrappy Queen

Our Incognito Queen

Our Enduring Queen (pre-order)

Our Indelible Queen (pre-order)

Our Broken Queen (pre-order)

Our Ageless Queen (pre-order)

Hollywood Lights (Pre-Order)

Billionaire Romance

Show Time (Securing Selyne)

Money Shot

Three Shot

Martini Shot

Long Shot

Grayson Enterprises Series

Bedding the Boss

Enticing the Ex

Tempting the Teacher

Wedding the Widow

Short Story Collections and Bundles

Animal Attraction 4-Story Collection

Vegas Nights 4-Story Collection

Last Stand Saloon 4-Story Collection

Instalove Bundle

Fated Mates of SpecOps Sierra

Paranormal Romance

Riding with the Kodiak

Wild Wolf

Cocky Cougar

Broken Bear

Wanted Wolf

Cursed Cougar

Banished Bear

<u>**Fated Mates of Fortune Falls**</u>

Paranormal Romance

The Bear's Wandering Mate

The Bear's Fearless Mate

The Bear's Exquisite Mate

The Bear's Resilient Mate

About the Author

USA Today Bestselling Author Kameron Claire writes stories with witty tongues, wicked needs, and wild deeds. Her paranormal and contemporary books emphasize strong female leads and the protective alpha males who know how to love and support kick-ass, take-charge women. Many of her books contain military veterans, boss babes, dominant men, and goofy K9 hijinks.

Find her everywhere via linktr.ee/kameronclaire
Signed Paperbacks and discounted eBook bundles are available exclusively on her store
Subscribe to the Witty, Wicked & Wild community and read all her books online for as little as $10 a month.

amazon.com/author/kameronclaire

goodreads.com/kameronclaire

bookbub.com/authors/kameron-claire

facebook.com/kameronclaireauthor

instagram.com/kameronclaire

tiktok.com/@kameronclaireauthor